Cover image: "*Testa anatomica*," Filippo Balbi (oil on wood, 1854). Digital image courtesy of the Wellcome Library, London, under Creative Commons licensing (CC-BY 4.0).
Design by Joan Macrino.

Lanternfish Press
22 N. 3rd Street
Philadelphia, PA 19106

lanternfishpress.com

Printed in the United States of America.
Library of Congress Control Number: 2014949500
ISBN: 978-1-941360-02-6

About the Au

Photo: Kimberly Kunda

Vikram Paralkar was born in Mumbai, India, where his fondest childhood memory is of a visit to a book fair with his parents. After completing medical school, he moved to the United States in 2005 and is now a hematologist and researcher at the University of Pennsylvania. His writing has been published in the *New England Journal of Medicine* and he is a recipient of the American Society of Hematology's Scholar Award. *The Afflictions* is his first book.
@VikramParalkar
vikramparalkar.com

The Afflictions

Vikram Paralkar

LANTERNFISH PRESS
Philadelphia, PA

安

I.

I was surprised, Máximo, to learn that you were an apothecary. I've been here for seventy years, and more apothecaries than I can count have visited the Central Library during that time, but none has ever wanted to become a librarian. You're also older, let me guess, forty perhaps, while the rest of us have been here since hair sprouted around our lips. Careful with those bookcases—they're a little rickety. I suggest walking along this wall.

As I was saying, this place is like a monastery. Children are dropped here by their parents, and they start by sweeping floors and scrubbing walls. Most of them never rise above that level. The few who learn to read and write usually become scribes: they bind books, make copies of treatises, take dictation from visiting scholars. Only the exceptional among them move on to become librarians. I don't think we need to put you through that menial labor, though. I read your treatise on disorders of the pineal gland. Careful, painstaking work.

Usually one of the younger librarians shows novices around the place, but in your case I thought I'd do it myself. I need to stretch my legs anyway. I'm confined to my room these days by physicians who think that lying in bed is going to delay my death. I've had a longer life than a man deserves, and now consumption is hurrying things along. Don't worry, I'm not burdening you with a secret. Everyone knows—they've been treating me like a glass vase. In any case, this is as good an excuse as any for me to disobey medical orders.

Come this way, and watch the step around the bend.

As you can see, we're constantly adding new wings and segments to the Library. If only you knew—well, I suppose you soon will—the number of ledgers we receive every day! Detailed accounts of war injuries, reports of epidemics, claims of new remedies, designs for curative amulets, recipes for plant extracts from every corner of the world, and we librarians have to find a way to catalog them all. The Library is just a mirror of the state of medicine outside its walls. You know better than I that diagnosis and cure grow more esoteric by the day. It's not enough to be a physician—now you must know alchemy and cartography. Even the traffic of the stars. How does one keep track of it all? As the knowledge contained in the Library grows, so does its disorganization. Very few people understand this.

You'll learn about the outer corridors and their contents in time. You haven't mentioned it, Máximo, but I'm sure you're dying to see the main hall, aren't you? Yes, I thought so. Unless you had good reason to access it in the past, you probably weren't allowed in. We used to be much more open, but then there was that madman—I'll tell you about him later—anyway, we've had to become very strict. We let people in only if they have letters from their patrons guaranteeing their scholarship. And sanity. After all, there is only one *Encyclopaedia medicinae*, and it's too valuable to risk.

Yes, Máximo is with me. You can let him in. No need to search him.

Ignore that guard. He's a buffoon. They're not hired for their intelligence, as you can see. I suppose you're used to this—people staring—but still. I've spoken to the other librarians and they won't treat you any differently because of your size.

The *Encyclopaedia* comprises three hundred and twenty-seven volumes, each with its own teak shelf and reading bench. If you choose to spend your life among books and scrolls, the smells of vellum and parchment will grow closer to your heart than those of food. Do you know how parchment is made? It's a skill every librarian here learns. We've all spent time in abattoirs, trying to find pelts that haven't been whipped or prodded, that don't have scars or tick bites or spots of disease. It's quite gruesome.

Look at this volume here, at its perfect spine, at the clean, beautiful words. There's nothing to remind you of how its pages once hung on a butcher's rack surrounded by giblets. The raw pelt is first washed and soaked in lime to strip off the hair—the smell is horrific, I tell you—and you have to stir it thrice a day for just the right number of days. Too much and it will tear. Then the pelt is stretched, and the pegs holding it are tightened a little every few days, until it's thin and dry and strong as a drum. Who knows how many animals went into the making of this *Encyclopaedia*? An *Encyclopaedia* of healing. Written on death.

But enough of that. Look how elegant this volume is. The binding, the margins, the shape of every letter. As I said, there is only one *Encyclopaedia medicinae*.

Amnesia inversa

The invalid with *Amnesia inversa* explains away the first memory lapses because they involve distant acquaintances: barbers and peddlers, innkeepers and tobacconists. But then the episodes become more frequent. Gatekeepers who once greeted the invalid by name now ask pointed questions about his purpose. Vendors from whom he purchased flour and salt each week claim they have never seen his face before. His neighbors' eyes no longer flicker with recognition at the sight of him, and his friends answer their doors with the polite, suspicious smiles one reserves for strangers. The sufferer tries amulets and tinctures, prayers and supplications, but the disease progresses, swallowing all those dear to him, until finally he awakens on the rumpled sheets of a baffled and affronted lover, and realizes that he has been wiped from all human memory.

Scattered across the shelves of the Central Library are reports written by physicians who, grasping the nature of the condition, transcribed the words of the invalids while they spoke and dispatched the manuscripts with all possible haste before their own memories could fade. These physicians, when questioned about the reports, identified the handwriting as their own but had no memory of having written them. Perhaps that is evidence enough for the existence of this disease.

The fate of invalids with *Amnesia inversa* remains unknown, for the very nature of the malady prevents them from being studied. There are at least three possibilities. Perhaps the invalids live at home in anonymity, strangers even to neighbors who see them every day of their lives. Or they take their own lives in despair, hoping that death will end the amnesia and allow their friends to mourn them. Or else they transform themselves into wanderers, filling their days with fleeting infatuations and camaraderies in towns that they leave under cover of night, ridding themselves of the need to be remembered.

安

Agricola's Disease

Agricola's Disease robs its victims of their hearing; within two years of its onset they become profoundly deaf. There is at first little to distinguish Agricola's from other afflictions that deaden the ear, but once the disease has advanced, an infallible test can separate it from the rest. Responsible physicians perform this test only on wealthy invalids, because a diagnosis of Agricola's Disease can drive its victims to penury.

The test is simple. The only elixir known to treat Agricola's Disease comes from alchemists in the East, who must swear on pain of death to safeguard the ancient recipe. Many otologists keep a minute quantity of this elixir in their safes, a dilution of one part to sixty thousand. To test for the disease, they place a single drop on the invalid's tongue. Most invalids hear nothing, but those with Agricola's Disease hear a whisper of sound, a soft breeze, that ebbs almost before it begins. The diagnosis is made.

The elixir is worth more by weight than any other substance on earth. Once a year small phials of the green liquid leave the Imperial Apothecary and cross the oceans in armed ships. When a ship reaches port, news of its arrival flies through the land. Merchants set up tents on the shore, and invalids of high birth arrive with pouches of gold, ready for the auction to begin.

When the Imperial auctioneer holds up his commodity, the invalids stack their bids on their tables. Within a few moments the auction ends, and the phials go to those with the biggest piles of gold. They pour the contents into their mouths and the world bursts open. The grumbling of thwarted merchants, the clinking of coins behind the auctioneer's desk, the cawing of gulls on the sand, the cries of fishwives hawking their catch, and the roar of the churning, frothing sea soak into their bones. The invalids fall to their knees, weeping.

And then the cure begins to fade. They plead for mercy, but Agricola's Disease drops them back into their oubliette.

Since the day an outraged God loosed the first afflictions on the earth, people with deafness have adapted to their state. But those with Agricola's Disease, once they taste the elixir, can never do so. They gamble away their lands and fortunes to drink it again. Desire for sound consumes them until the remedy becomes as much a part of their misfortune as the malady itself.

Many of our own alchemists have tried to distill this elixir. The recipe remains elusive, but we are learning some of its properties. It appears to contain an almost endless number of vital essences, mixed in proportions that correspond to the full range of human hearing. At the latest tally, over three thousand of these have been identified—some that restore the invalid's ability to hear the wings of sparrows, others that cover the lower sonorities of dulcimers, yet others that are concerned with the sounds of raindrops. Buried deep within the concoction are the more complex essences governing speech. Some open the ears to the voices of priests, some to those of barbers, some to the words of madmen.

Immortalitas diabolica

Immortalitas diabolica is poorly documented, for no one will admit to suffering from it. The authorities become suspicious, however, when villages whisper of an inhabitant with obscene youthfulness, free of the illnesses and deformities that have visited everyone else his age.

Immortalitas diabolica grants its victims the ability to will away every pain and infirmity that befalls them. The ability first surfaces in childhood, when the instantaneous cure of scrapes and fevers seems as natural to them as speaking. As they grow, they see those around them suffer through illnesses that they themselves can dispel with a fleeting thought. They acquire a reputation for remarkable health, but it is not until the fourth and fifth decades of their lives that people around them question their pristine skin, their robust teeth, their luminous hair.

It is usually then that the invalid learns the terrible truth about his health. *Immortalitas diabolica* does not cure afflictions—it transfers them to the bodies of others. When a person with this power reaches within himself to expunge his illness, its vapors leave his body and settle on some innocent passerby, who must now suffer an illness fate has not ordained for him. As the person with *Immortalitas diabolica* ages, the legacy of the gift weighs heavier upon him, and while he can effortlessly banish diseases that threaten his body, he cannot banish the memories of those whose lives he has blighted.

Some people with *Immortalitas diabolica* try to reject the gift, allowing wrinkles to line their faces, scars to riddle their lungs, cancers to flourish in their guts. But when the terminal moments of agony and suffocation arrive, Lucifer rages in their minds. Intoxicated with pain, they stagger then into dingy alleys, to the huts of the poor and destitute who are unlikely to be missed, and they allow themselves to drink from the monstrous elixir that swirls within. When the deed is done, their young, muscular legs whisk them away as cries emerge from the windows beside which they stood.

Nevertheless, those cursed with *Immortalitas diabolica* are not truly immortal. After extraordinarily long lives, they die of causes unknown. Necropsy reveals youthful, supple tissues, a body that appears to have expired at the peak of health. Spasms of the heart, poisons in the blood, or other fatal chances too sudden to be wished away may lie behind these deaths, but some authorities suggest that the mechanism is not so simple. They posit that sickness and suffering are integral to the human soul, so a person with *Immortalitas diabolica* must forsake fragments of his soul each time he expunges an illness. It is then only a matter of time before the soul is ground to dust, and all that is left is a body in pristine repair, devoid of any vital force to sustain it.

Libertine's Disease

Libertine's Disease first appears in the writings of a Majorcan abbot whose missionary excursions to the docks taught him a great deal about man's baser proclivities. It was not mere naïve shock at the ways of the world, then, that caused him to describe a peculiar epidemic, which "drives wench and sailor alike to a feverish degree of wickedness, unheard of even among these classes, deficient in modesty and piety." In his journals he wrote that they possessed "the urge to sin with such unholy fervor that they sometimes take to bed two or even three others possessed with the same unquenchable thirst." The papers he left behind in the monastery mention also his fruitless attempts to treat this witchery with infusions of chasteberry and rue.

Libertine's Disease is unique among the myriad contagions transmitted through carnal exchange, for it is the only one known to alter the very urges of its hosts to speed its own propagation. It produces what some call *pruritus profanus*—the profane itch, relieved by sexual congress but returning to torment the invalid even before the languor of the act has subsided. Those with many lovers are most vulnerable to infection, but the disease can drive even the chaste into a state of ravenous lust, transforming them quite against their wills into libertines. A variety of texts both ancient and modern speak of infamous seducers, whose catalogs of conquests numbered into the thousands. In all likelihood they were victims of the ailment, which drove them to feats beyond the reach of simple adulterers, whose virility and lust are merely human.

Extracts of scorzonera and nenuphar, applied twice a day to the privy parts, are effective against this affliction and can cure it within a fortnight.

Libertine's Disease, however, perverts not only the sexual desires of its hosts but also their beliefs. By mechanisms that remain poorly understood, it can undo a lifetime of Christian righteousness and replace it with idolatry of the flesh and the worship of carnal, pagan gods. Its victims then reject all treatments as heresy.

The disease has kindled the interest of our apothecaries, who now attempt to extract its vital essences for use in diluted form as aphrodisiacs. Experiments on willing volunteers have not yielded encouraging results, however. The tinctures have a complex and delicate balance, and the slightest error can result in the accidental conversion of the subject into a lifelong celibate.

Mors inevitabilis

Mors inevitabilis, or Inevitable Death, was first described half a century ago, but the medical fraternity has learned little more about it in the years since. The exact processes by which the invalids reach their fatal ends within a year of diagnosis remain as opaque as ever.

The disease is an insidious one. Few can distinguish its early stages from the morbid musings that flit through every human mind from time to time. But the thoughts of the invalid differ in subtle ways from those of other men. The person with *Mors inevitabilis* contemplates neither the moment of his potential death nor the manner in which he might reach it, but rather fixates on the actual substance of death, the nature and texture of death, the sensation of death. As the affliction progresses, this contemplation yields to a growing acceptance of the prospect of mortality, so familiar has the touch and taste of it become to his mind. At no point does the invalid exhibit any impulse to end his life. It is vital for the physician to distinguish *Mors inevitabilis* from the fatalisms that can torment even resilient men into craving, and achieving through condemnable devices, the darkness of eternal rest.

Once the acceptance of death has taken hold, the invalid grows convinced of his own approaching end and begins to speak openly of it. Despite growing awareness of this disease among men of medicine, invalids at this stage are often shackled in asylums by misguided practitioners hoping to shield them from self-harm. But even in the final stages, those with *Mors inevitabilis* lead robust, vigorous lives without a trace of despair. A year after the first signs, they reach an acceptance so deep and peaceful that their souls drift free of their bodies without protest.

A vast majority of those who succumb to *Mors inevitabilis* are youths of great capacity and promise. While their loss is tragic, it is softened by the dignity of their passage, a quality lacking in the demise of most men. One is therefore tempted to question why a just and benevolent God, who decreed that death be a basic term in the treaty of earthly existence, should deny the rest of mankind such a pure and tranquil transition into the afterlife, instead choosing to infuse the final moments with delirium, torment, and blood.

Lingua fracta

It is at first difficult to distinguish *Lingua fracta* from more conventional aphasias. Its victims find their vocabularies grossly shrunken—but the patterns of loss depend on their native language. Speakers of English always keep the use of *root, bath,* and *tender* but lose *song, pilgrim,* and *vex.* French invalids lose *chaud, livre,* and *jambe* but keep *rue, très,* and *maintenant.* German speakers retain *Antwort, Farbe,* and *Musik* but not *nie, träumen, Gebeine.* Grammar also suffers. Depending on their native tongue, invalids find themselves unable to conjugate a verb in the present tense, or to join two clauses with a conjunction, or to use an adjective. *Lingua fracta* does not spare languages of hand signs, making it clear that the disease cuts deep into the substrate of language.

The set of words lost is distinct in every language, without overlap. Only speakers of Arabic retain a word for birth, while only the Dutch have one for death. After decades of study, the Guild of Linguists has assembled all these leftover words into a single dissonant, bristling tongue that is capable of almost a full range of expression. But even this chimeric language remains incomplete. They are now turning to extinct languages printed on tablets and papyrus scrolls, mining them for words that no one alive has ever pronounced.

The medical uses of the chimeric tongue are limited. In order to be fluent, one would have to master all the world's languages, but few victims of *Lingua fracta* can learn even the rudiments of a handful of them. The only ones able to converse are linguists of the highest rank, those with mastery of a thousand dialects. These master linguists argue that *Lingua fracta* does not deprive its victims of language at all, but rather allows them to rediscover a lost primordial tongue. This, they believe, is none other than the Adamic language, the language of God Himself, last uttered at the Tower of Babel.

Vulnus morale

The wound of *Vulnus morale,* or the Moral Wound, begins in adolescence as a round ulceration on the small of the back. At first there is little to distinguish it from the most harmless of ulcers, and village healers may poultice it with herbs and salves for years. But sooner or later the ulcer expands into a large, unsightly wound, and the invalid turns to a more learned healer.

The diagnostic process is long and tedious, and can take the most skilled physician the better part of a year. The sufferer must document the state of his conscience in a ledger: every act of kindness or malice, every bitter word, every stolen candlestick, every coin tossed on the mat of a pauper. He must keep track not only of his deeds, but also his thoughts: resentment towards his master, jealousy of his brother, the thunderous lust that soaks him at the sight of a forbidden person. Deeper and deeper he must dig, until he has spilled on paper the regions of his mind that he keeps hidden even in the confessional. The physician wades though this morass of turpitude and uses equations written by the moralists of old to approximate the infinitely more complex tallies kept in the divine ledgers. Only after months of this humiliating exercise do patterns emerge. Correlations appear between wound and ledger. A subtle shrinkage of the ulcer can be matched with a period of charity, the sudden appearance of necrosis with a fit of murderous rage.

The invalid with *Vulnus morale* bears on his back a permanent compass of his moral state. Men who spend lives of great evil are converted into horrific tapestries of slough and gangrene that narrate their terrible deeds. The priest who arrives at the hour of death to commend such a man's soul to the mercy of God finds his voice ringing false. But there are others who, after long years of debauchery, return in the twilight of their lives to the practice of humility and virtue. By the time they depart from this mortal world, their rapidly cooling skins are as smooth and immaculate as on the day of their birth.

Pulchritudo scelerata

Pulchritudo scelerata, or Accursed Beauty, grants its victims a bewitching loveliness. As people with this condition flower into youth, word of their perfection spreads far and wide. Only then does the malevolence of the disease manifest itself. The age of eighteen brings with it the pathologies that have earned this malady its place in the *Encyclopaedia*.

Anyone who lays eyes on the person with *Pulchritudo scelerata* will suffer migraines, catarrh, evanescent rashes, and inflammations of the joints and sinuses—manifestations subtle and transient enough to escape the notice of even the most astute physicians. However, the pathologies accumulate, and those who are habitually exposed find themselves prostrated by more distressing afflictions: tumors of the jaw, abscesses in the spine, atrophy of the limbs. The town's physicians, overwhelmed by the storm of infirmities, at last recognize the pattern: almost all the victims are lovelorn youths who have spent long stretches of time gazing through window shutters and tree branches at the beauty of a neighborhood damsel, the source of all their ills.

The authorities condemn those diagnosed with *Pulchritudo scelerata* to a lifetime behind masks and veils, unless they agree to scar their faces to the point of disfigurement, thus neutralizing the venom. But there are many who cannot accept either of these choices. They flee their homes and turn into itinerants, pausing in remote towns where the unsuspecting inhabitants fall mute in adoration, then moving on so as not to leave permanent scars by their presence. The authorities panic when a scattering of afflictions breaks out in the wake of a mysterious traveler, but there is little they can do to contain the invalid who has long since fled. Superstitions about this disease abound. A sketch of the escaped invalid, posted in the town square to warn people, could prevent the malady almost entirely. But no town will hang one for fear that the arresting face looking out of the image might itself be capable of harm.

Erysifia Poisoning

The mind is vulnerable to an astonishing range of poisons and toxins, and nature produces such substances freely. But even among the most notorious of these, *Erysifia* holds a unique position. Its true properties were first described by a Cathayan alchemist who, during a visit to a tea plantation, wandered off the road while handpicking leaves for his morning cup. Had he cared to show his leaves to the workers, he would have learned of his error, but instead he returned to his cottage and added them to a boiling kettle, thus unwittingly brewing a concentrated draught of *Erysifia.*

The alchemist documented the ensuing horrors in a treatise that has now been translated. He described the effect of *Erysifia* as "an experience of utmost oppression. The nausea and disorientation it caused were beyond belief. For weeks I saw and heard and perceived things that allowed me neither calm nor slumber nor appetite. *Erysifia* poisoned my every happiness, and I was plunged into something immeasurably worse than despair." The effects of the extract, already well known to the common folk of those areas, thus came to the attention of the medical fraternity.

Erysifia is often confused with truth potions. The latter loosen the tongues of their victims into revealing secrets never meant to be repeated. *Erysifia* does the exact opposite: it makes the invalid unable to perceive anything but absolute, undiluted truth. *Erysifia* strips the mind of the devices it normally uses to fortify itself against the world. For months, the victim cannot help but stare at all the petty vengeances plotted by those around him, the dissonances of their thoughts, their hypocrisies, their lusts. He is forced to see those he loves not as he wishes them to be, but as they really are. In cases of severe poisoning, *Erysifia* turns the victim's gaze upon himself, making him witness to the horrors of his own soul. At this extremity, the poison can destroy the mind. The only recorded deaths from *Erysifia* are suicides.

The alchemist's treatise ends thus: "We all believe that illumination would give us pleasure. But none of us dares look straight into the noonday sun."

In certain tribes of the Far East all children are given tiny doses of *Erysifia* right from infancy, and all adults drink infusions of its leaves. Three explanations exist for this: that these tribal people are immune to the drug; that they too suffer from its effects but use it as a ritual means of penance and flagellation; or that consuming it from infancy grants them the ability to move beyond the ugly truths that *Erysifia* first reveals, and to gaze instead on the deeper truths of life itself, which are surely exquisite to behold.

Forma cyclica

Men who suffer from *Forma cyclica* lead bisected lives. The daily rhythm of the disease changes them into specimens of physical perfection at noon, then into the coarsest hunchbacks at midnight. The next day, the rising sun promises renewed handsomeness and symmetry. Women have rhythms opposite to those of men. In darkness, in candlelight, they are radiant; yet they cannot forget the crumpled faces and deformed bodies that await them in the day.

At the peak of their beauty, these invalids can seduce anyone they fancy. They must, however, seduce in haste, for the beauty is short-lived. When they feel their looks waning, they flee and hide while their tissues suffer the hours of disfigurement.

The nature of the illness prevents those with *Forma cyclica* from finding companionship in the world of the healthy. Those whose features are static can never reconcile the invalid of the day with the invalid of the night. The sufferers therefore turn to others with the same disease for consolation. They join in communions of shared affliction, using masks and cloaks to cover their own defects while admiring the splendors of the other. Their intimacies are restricted to dawn and dusk, when neither of them is beautiful, but neither is hideous.

As the invalids age, the cycles grow erratic. Sometimes their beauty lasts for days, or it may disappear for long stretches. They may go through an entire day's cycle in an hour. Many such invalids turn into recluses. Some lift their veils only in brief moments of perfection, gaining reputations as shy beauties. Others, in defiance of the world and its judgments, unveil themselves precisely at their nadir.

Only with death does the cycling stop. Too many of these invalids worry about where in the cycle they will be at the precise moment of their passing—what mourners will see at the funeral. The wiser among them know that the soul has no physical form, no beauty and no ugliness. Loosed from their fickle bodies, it will remain forever constant.

II.

You know, Máximo, as a child, I wanted to become an apothecary myself.

That was before I was brought to this Library. I don't remember my parents. I was raised by an aunt who, truth be told, couldn't wait for me to grow up, so she could throw me out of her house with a clean conscience. I must have been six when a horse-drawn caravan laden with strange objects pulled into the town square. It was a traveling apothecary. I had never seen such a spectacle.

For three days the townsfolk visited the apothecary with all the woes of their bodies and minds. There were grandfathers with aching knees, young women with barren wombs, mothers whose sons were in love with disagreeable maidens. The apothecary had medicines for them all.

I would stand in the crowd and stare at the apothecary's bottles for hours, fascinated by the way his hands could turn mere weeds and minerals into remedies. On the fourth day, after the town's needs had been met, the apothecary packed up his caravan. His apprentice tethered it to the horses, and they rattled away down the road. It was afternoon when they reached the next town, where a new sea of villagers flocked to them. Anticipating an evening of good business, the apothecary opened the doors of the caravan. There, asleep in the midst of his bottles, was a little boy.

That was me! The moment the caravan pulled into my town, I had decided to run away from home and become a man of medicine. I wanted this apothecary to take me under his wing and train me as his apprentice. But he was a dour man with no interest in children. He twisted my ear and dragged me out. Then he flogged his horses all the way back to my town. He deposited me with my aunt, who did her part by flogging me.

It's amusing now to think back to that time. I remember sitting inside the caravan, listening to the jars rattle in rhythm to the clops of the horses' hooves. I remember wondering how the difference between health and disease could be contained in such tiny bottles. In one state, man is free to walk and speak. In the other he's flat on the ground. How can a red liquid correct this difference?

Even now I marvel that two substances, when mixed, can lose their individual qualities and become a third substance that is entirely new. It makes me wonder what we'd find if we could distill a human being. How many elements, mixed in what proportions?

Would one of those be the element of the soul? And could you distill even that one further?

But I was just six at the time of my adventure, and I'm sure I wasn't capable then of such lofty thoughts. The traveling apothecary returned to our town every year, and every year I tried to run away with him. Then one year he told my aunt about the Central Library and its constant need for young apprentices. She paid him to take me off her hands and drop me here.

So I have an apothecary to thank for making me a Librarian. It's a long story, Máximo, but I hope it answers your question about why I'm going out of my way to show you the *Encyclopaedia* in such detail.

Renascentia

For most of the year, invalids with *Renascentia* suffer their various ailments quietly, but when the spring equinox approaches their emotions outweigh every symptom. Churches nail the exact day and hour of the equinox to their doors. The anxious sufferers gather there far ahead of time. Some wheeze through congested lungs, others writhe in pain, and still others limp on atrophied legs, while a few show no outward signs of disease at all. On the morning of the equinox the doors creak open and naves fill to suffocation with both the robust and the decrepit.

As the moment draws close their voices rise. Sobs and moans echo from the walls. The scene is ghastly to witness, a theater of man's humiliation before an unmoved God. And then the equinox passes, and the crowds stagger out. They test the strength of their legs, examine themselves for the effects of *Renascentia*.

Some leave with freshly pockmarked faces, others with new obstructions of their bowels. Some receive dementias or epilepsies or fulminant afflictions that wrack them with agony even as they rise from the pews. And others are cured of consumption. Their amputated limbs grow back, or their pustules vanish. They weep with relief, avoiding the eyes of those condemned in the rationing—but soon they begin to worry about unseen tumors implanted within them, waiting to blossom.

Renascentia, or Rebirth, is a disease of the celestial cycle. Each spring brings with it a casting of the divine dice: a new palette of ills or cures for those who survived the previous year. Physicians have tried to find patterns in the disease, but *Renascentia* seems to follow no rules. No one can predict its reaping.

Some theoreticians suggest that *Renascentia* is no crueler than life itself. Every man has his cycles of health and disease. For those afflicted with *Renascentia,* the cycling is simply more rapid. A few theologians even take this argument to its extreme. They claim that *Renascentia,* by giving sufferers an equal chance each year at poison and antidote, is a glimpse of God at His fairest.

Bernard's Malady

The first traces of Bernard's Malady appear in the squalid outskirts of our cities. People who have lived their whole lives on the edge of starvation develop vivid memories of a time when they gorged on extravagant meals. Beggars who have never known anything but a hut with a dirt floor remember mansions with silver cutlery and curtains spun from golden thread. Poor women pounding grain in their hovels, surrounded by a squabbling brood, speak with fondness of the grand halls and chateaux in which they were raised.

And at once the invalids cannot stand the stenches to which they had grown accustomed. Their eyes thirst for lace and brocade and find the sight of their own dingy homes revolting. They refuse to work at the honest jobs they were once grateful to have, believing manual labor to be beneath their dignity. Some even resort to thievery in the desire to reclaim the wealth that is their birthright.

The disease soon creeps into airier neighborhoods until it reaches even the doorsteps of the rich. Merchants believe themselves to be feudal vassals, knights puff themselves up into noblemen, dukes remember how they once sat on thrones. Kingdoms can crumble unless these lordly sufferers are quarantined in dungeons. No king has yet suffered from the malady, and thankfully so, for it might well drive him to wage war against the heavens.

Scholars argue that the mechanism behind this affliction is the same one that produces disfiguring scars at the sites of trifling injuries. Unable to alter the present, Bernard's Malady alters the past. Unable to repair the iniquities of the visible world, it repairs the fabric of memory. But it succeeds only in magnifying misery though the lens of false opulence.

Tristitia contagiosa

Only recently did the medical fraternity recognize *Tristitia contagiosa,* or Contagious Melancholy, as a real disease, though even the ancient Greeks knew that foul breath could transmit sadness. Its corpuscles reside in the lungs and can easily spread from person to person, setting off epidemics.

The first victims hurry to the taverns, hoping to drink away their sorrows. There they spread the contagion to all those around them, until the alcohol is exhausted and the sufferers stagger into the world.

They infect the jesters, the blacksmiths, even the fishermen down at the wharfs. Drunk on melancholy, men lie abed, children stop their games, women lock themselves in sculleries.

But there are some whom the disease spurs into expression. Poets sing of lost hopes and decaying romances. Composers fill scores with lamentations. Painters spill anguish across their canvases.

At last the epidemic spends itself, and the town returns to ordinary life. The elders decree that any works created during the period of affliction be destroyed, fearing that the vapors of contagion might lie dormant in the bleak creations. Bonfires burn in every town square as the dark masterpieces, like heretics, are silenced. With the last traces of the disease destroyed, the town forces itself to forget the episode.

Accounts of the time of contagion, even from the town's trusted historians, are unreliable. Historians are not immune to infection, and their reports are filtered through the melancholy in their own hearts. Our best understanding of the disease comes from the rare works of art that escape the incinerations and find their way to the outside world. It is unknown whether the corpuscles of *Tristitia* can truly linger in such works. But one must be careful, for they work a change in at least some viewers, whose souls grow melancholy as they head for the nearest tavern.

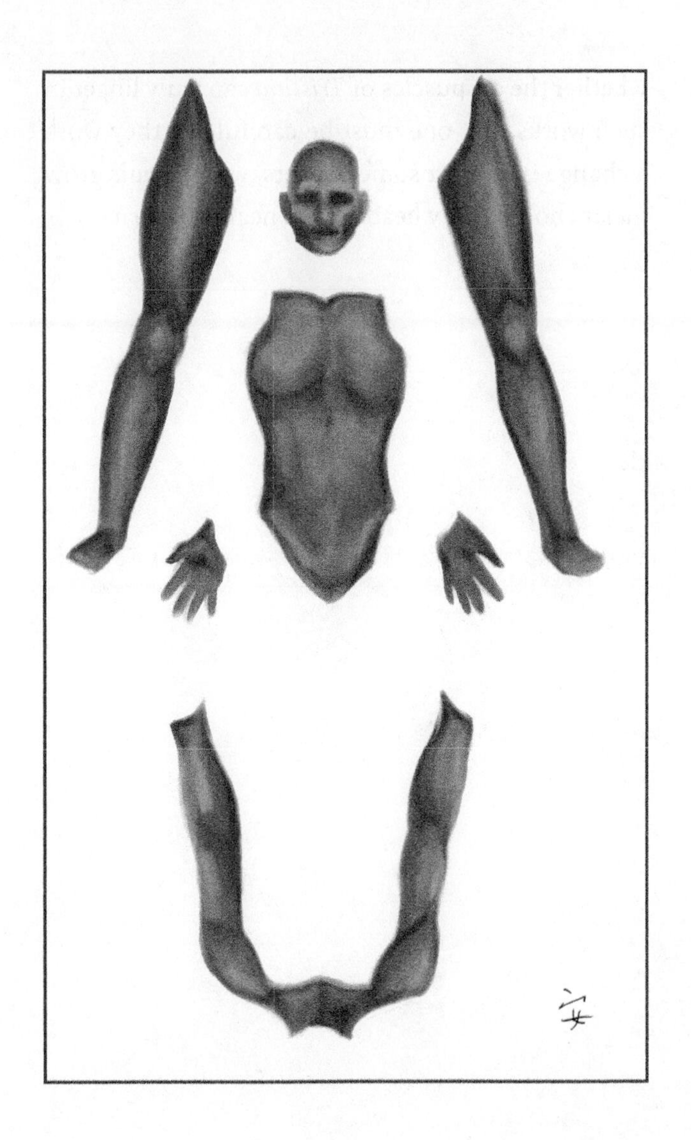
安

Corpus ambiguum

While many afflictions produce fixed and predictable derangements of sensation, the delusions of *Corpus ambiguum* are always shifting. Only with great effort can its victims recognize their skins as the boundaries of their bodies. The slightest distraction makes them lose the sense of where their bodies end and the surrounding world begins. On being asked to sketch pictures of themselves, invalids with this condition often draw incomplete versions of their own bodies, surrounded by amorphous auras and clouds of disjointed appendages.

Or they may give themselves features borrowed from those around them: secret moles, hidden rashes, surgical scars, inverted nipples. They may reach out and touch, with casual nonchalance, the private areas of other people's anatomy.

Cases both tragic and fascinating occur in the medical literature. In a moment of intense fear, one woman with *Corpus ambiguum* bludgeoned her own leg to a pulp, convinced that it belonged to an intruder. There was a man who, in the throes of sexual intercourse, would experience tremendous pleasure during his wife's spasms, yet feel nothing at his own moment of climax. And there is one well-documented case of a woman who managed to bend the disease to her will. She took up the study of anatomy and became a healer. By laying hands on invalids she would sense their pain, identify their pathologies, even manipulate their organs into expelling the stones and cysts that had laid them low.

Then she began to expel demons from epileptics. The local priests resented this intrusion into their domain and accused her of witchcraft. She fled the place, leaving the townsfolk to the privacy of their own afflictions.

Mors transiens

The first documented case of *Mors transiens* was a man who awoke from an episode of deep oblivion to find himself trapped inside a suffocating box. His cries filled the mourners at his funeral with terror. When they gathered their wits and pried open the coffin, they found the deceased man alive within it, mad with fear. The cold clammy lips upon which his widow had planted a last trembling kiss were warm and animated again.

The agent that provokes this disease remains unidentified. There are other afflictions that cause their sufferers to slip into a premature likeness of death. But *Mors transiens* goes beyond mere simulation of death, and therein lies its terrible essence.

During an episode the invalid is, by all definitions known to medicine, a cadaver. The heart ceases to beat, the nerves grow inert, the blood congeals within the veins, and the lungs deflate and fill with fluid. Unable to maintain their store of sustaining heat, the muscles stiffen rapidly, and the body cools. There have been cases in which the corpses of the afflicted proceeded far past mottling of the skin and demonstrated clear signs of putrefaction.

There is in fact no means of distinguishing an episode of *Mors transiens* from death itself. The diagnosis can only be made in retrospect, when the corruption of the flesh is abruptly reversed and all of the processes of the mind and body are restored, to the understandable shock of all present.

Rare though the affliction is, it has gripped the imagination of the populace like no other. Lovers now weep beside the corpses of their beloved not just from grief but from desperate hope, and even the morticians who eventually tear them away from the coffins do so with hesitation, for few would wish to have their vocation tarnished forever with accusations of murder. Embalmers are now in great demand, for mourners whose purses are deep enough to permit extravagances want their deceased preserved in careful concoctions of rare spirits. They greet the taut, perfumed mummies each day with futile longings shimmering in their eyes.

The tremendous distress that this disease inflicts on mourners is unquestionable. The trauma it inflicts on the rich history of intellectual accomplishment is less acknowledged, yet every bit as pernicious. *Mors transiens* has poisoned with doubt what was once an immutable given. By stripping humanity of the fundamental absolute of civilization, *Mors transiens* threatens, in one fell stroke, to topple the magnificent edifice of philosophy, art and literature, which has rested on the finality of death since the day Eve ate of the forbidden fruit.

Persona fracta

Persona fracta, or Broken Identity, should interest all those who study the integrity of the human form, but owing to its generally harmless nature, it has rarely garnered the attention of the medical fraternity. However, in recent years there have been increasing reports of the disease, all showing a striking concordance of symptomatology. It is therefore worthy of mention in the *Encyclopaedia*.

A seamstress diagnosed with *Persona fracta* was unable to think of the 'she' who walked and the 'she' who spoke as the same individual. She was even unable to reconcile the 'she' who walked with the 'she' who ran, or the 'she' who spoke with the 'she' who whispered, for in her mind, when her limbs and lungs and throat engaged in different actions, they were governed by different persons, each with a specific faculty, each performing her function and then receding into dormancy when her services were no longer needed. There were of course persons who were perpetually at the fore—the 'she' who breathed, the 'she' who smelt, the 'she' who ached.

Some classify this condition as a mental derangement, but *Persona fracta* has features that ordinary insanity cannot explain. Although this seamstress had never been schooled in the sciences, she possessed a remarkable understanding of the human form and could speak in great detail of the 'she' who pushed vital fluids through the channels of the body, the 'she' who worked night and day to cleanse and redden the blood, the 'she' who cushioned the bones as they ground against one another, the 'she' who, until recently, possessed the cyclical ability to bear children. She even spoke poignantly of the treacherous 'she' who had nearly killed her, and her eyes misted as she recalled an inflammation of the liver from a decade earlier.

The harmonious fashion in which these identities cooperate with each other, until the natural death of the invalid from entirely other causes, has led many to classify the condition as a curiosity rather than a disease. But there are theologians who see in *Persona fracta* the first sparks of a dangerous heresy. While most men rightly understand their bodies to be vessels for their singular and indivisible souls, *Persona fracta* deceives its victims into believing that the soul too is made of fragments, hanging together at the mercy of mortal flesh and destined to perish with it. Thus the disease may well have a fatal effect, that of jeopardizing the eternal salvation of its victims.

Foetus perfidus

Of the many diseases of pregnancy, *Foetus perfidus* is perhaps the rarest and strangest. Despite much study, it continues to baffle physicians and philosophers alike, and in essence belongs to a category of its own.

The conception itself is unremarkable, and all examination suggests the presence of a fetus developing in the expected fashion. But as late as the seventh month, *Foetus perfidus* may manifest itself, first halting the growth of the fetus, then reversing it. The woman finds her abdomen deflating as the cranium of the fetus shrinks and its motions weaken. The listener who places an ear on her stretched skin hears the heartbeats growing frail and distant, until they are silenced. The rest of the disease is hidden from inquiry, and the womb, after a period of regression equal to the period of gestation, is restored to its original state.

All attempts to deliver a viable fetus at the first sign of the disease have failed, for it continues to shrink outside the uterus, until the clumsy instruments of men can no longer support its delicate functions and it suffocates.

After much debate, the guilds of physicians have agreed that the most merciful way of addressing *Foetus perfidus* is to allow the disease to take its course. Though this inflicts anguish on the mother, for whom the affliction is equivalent to a protracted miscarriage, most women accept it as preferable to the alternative. They allow the fetus to regress undisturbed inside them and complete the painless, peaceful arc of its life within the warmth of a womb it will never leave.

Aphasia floriloquens

Aphasia floriloquens is difficult to place among the ninety-two categories of linguistic derangements known to man, for it is the only aphasia marked by an extraordinary *excess* of speech, rather than a lack of it. The invalid with *Aphasia floriloquens,* wishing to send a letter, walks into a post office and launches into a dissertation on the history of mail, ranging over such topics as the ancient epistles sent from Syria to Babylon, the carriage routes established by Omodeo Tasso, the inscriptions on rolls of papyrus transported down the rivers of northern Africa, the scroll dispatched by Fabricius to Pyrrhus alerting the latter to an assassination attempt on his royal person, the clay tablets used on the Phoenician shore to communicate crop yields, and the sinking of a postal ship off the coast of Arborea. Yet he finds himself absolutely incapable of uttering the simple sentence, "I wish to send a letter."

The invalid turns in desperation to the library, studying thick volumes with scholarly zeal in an attempt to learn words and facts that might help him communicate, but instead he becomes lost in the morass of his own scholarship. When asked about apiaries, he rambles eruditely on the feeding habits of spiders. When questioned about the dimensions of ship hulls, he discourses on the salinity of oceans.

These invalids are often exploited. The curious persuade them to give public lectures, which are like the traveling carnivals that display men with bodily deformities. Their lectures are immensely popular. The invalid with *Aphasia floriloquens* stands on a stage spluttering, vainly struggling to answer the simple questions posed to him, while hundreds of learned men sit alert with their quills and papers, hoping to extract a few brilliant juxtapositions from the web of arcane tangents. The whole world lines up to hear the torrent of words that the disease inspires, yet the invalid's own thoughts and lamentations pass unheard.

Exilium volatile

When ships sail over the broadest expanses of ocean, their passengers become vulnerable to *Exilium volatile,* or Transient Exile. The vapors of the disease bubble up from depths that even monsters fear, engulfing vessels unfortunate enough to be passing overhead at the precise moment when they break the surface. Travelers breathe the vapors, and the affliction begins.

Suspended between blank horizons, the travelers weep as if severed from their homes forever, even if they had every intention of returning to their native lands. The bonds that tied them to their own plains and valleys are snapped, and they suffer the pangs of collective exile. Drifting for what seems like eternity between the harbors they inhabited and those to which they are bound, their minds grow estranged from caftan or cravat, from spice or stew, from tower or thatch. They grieve for foods whose tastes have vanished from their tongues, lovers whose faces are turned away from them, languages whose cadences they no longer remember. In the loneliness of the voyage, in the throes of *Exilium,* they grope for memories that might lend them some sense of belonging, but unable to find any, they believe for a terrible instant that the sum of their existence lies confined within the ship that carries them.

As the ship advances and the vapors dissipate, the minds of the travelers grow calm. They feel the pull of the earth again as their vessel approaches its harbor, and an affinity blossoms within them for a culture they have never known. They thirst for music they have never heard, cuisines they have never tasted, landscapes they have never seen. By the time they alight from the vessel, the alienation of *Exilium volatile* has subsided completely, and the travelers find themselves transformed into instant natives of the new land, their loves and loyalties now anchored there. Those who had left families and children behind think of them as phantasms, remnants of a dream they wish to forget.

There are some however whose lungs the vapors of *Exilium* never leave. These travelers continue to feel on earth the same suffocating alienation they felt at sea. Unable to feel any attachment for the port on which they now stand, they return to the land of their birth, only to find that the streets and spires and kinsmen with whom they were raised seem distant and unfamiliar. They travel to other lands, attempting to blend with the locals by adopting their garments, imbibing their liquors, reciting their hymns—but the search is fruitless. The disease is then termed *Exilium perpetuum*, a variant in which the travelers are condemned to a lifetime of exile, wandering in perpetual search of an unattainable comfort, their worn-out baggage serving as the only constant in their nomadic lives.

III.

You'll forgive me for venturing into personal matters here, Máximo, but let me share my admiration for you. It can't be easy being a dwarf, and suffering from your kind of facial deformity—I hope you don't mind me using that word—yet you have come so far. The man on the street doesn't understand these things. He's quick to label someone a monster and move on without bothering to look for the man within the body. We librarians aren't like that. No, not at all.

Diseases of children, especially those that begin in the womb, have always perplexed me. What possible purpose could they serve? What divine design? There's a section of the Library full of fetuses pickled in preserving liquid. Some of them have two heads, others have a single eye, others have gills in their necks. There are speculations about the mechanisms behind such defects—you'll find plenty in this *Encyclopaedia*—but none that ever satisfy me.

We all carry within us the original sin of Adam. Why does one man carry it deep within, hidden from all the world, while another must show it on his face?

If this parchment I'm holding had ended up in an abbey, monks would have slaved over it, colored it with gold leaf and tempera, drawn winged seraphs in the margins, and set filigreed vines and arabesques trailing from every letter. All to depict the glory of God's creation. Instead, the parchment finds itself here, in this volume, where austere men of medicine force it to describe an awful affliction.

Let me tell you this: my Library welcomes you. As long as I am Head Librarian—as long as my name holds any sway in the corridors of this Library—no one will treat you any differently. If they do, tell them, "Senhor José would be ashamed of you." That will shut their mouths.

The Curse of Sisyphus

The progress of the Curse of Sisyphus is quite unmistakable. Once it has been diagnosed, the physician faces the unpleasant task of informing the family that the disease is incurable, that all intervention is futile, and that their offspring will require lifelong care.

In the second year of life, a toddler who has thus far developed normally loses all the skills it has painstakingly acquired and is reduced in every aspect, except bodily size, to the state of a newborn. He forgets the voice and touch of his mother and peers at the world with unfocused eyes. The grasping fingers retain their developed structure, but their motions become primitive, as do those of the legs, which lose the craft of balance and locomotion. The child stops speaking, unable to do anything with its mouth besides cry and suckle.

Then begins a long process of relearning. The regressed toddler can gradually reacquire the ability to smile, to crawl, to babble. It regains emotion and imitation, and learns again to trust the firmness of its legs and the grip of its fingers. While these encouraging signs give hope to parents and caretakers, the grim prognosis is ordained at the first episode of regression. The hourglass turns again when two more years have elapsed. The invalid's mind, now housed in the body of a four-year-old, returns to the moment of birth, whence the futile climb resumes.

The Curse of Sisyphus continues to perplex the medical fraternity, even as those who suffer from it age into helpless antiquity and succumb finally to the diseases of their senescent bodies. Theologians and moralists have attempted to fill the void by positing a controversial theory. They suggest that the point of reversal, the second year of life, represents the age at which humans learn to commit the venial sins of defiance and insolence, thus laying the foundation for later, more deadly transgressions. They argue that the Curse of Sisyphus represents the soul's attempt to reject the sin that condemned its progenitors: it is a refusal to bite into the apple of earthly growth and knowledge, an attempt to undo the fall of man. The invalid, his mortal climb thwarted so many times, is therefore assured after death of an unobstructed ascent to the highest heavens.

Tabes arcana

The bodies of those with *Tabes arcana,* or Mysterious Decay, constantly teeter at the edge of dissolution, and only by force of will can the invalids sustain the integrity of their tissues. Once touched by the affliction, their bodies become susceptible to the corruption of death even as they speak and breathe.

The typical invalid may find his arm growing cold and insensate for no reason. Without intervention, the limb would darken and desiccate into a useless twig. But the invalid calms his panic and recites the hymns his physician has taught him. As he recites, warmth and vitality return to the numb limb and its sinews, as though they had never known the threat of gangrene.

The ancient texts that first make mention of this illness list strings of syllables that the invalid must recite with great precision for the healing to be accomplished. These "hymns," for so we call them, are specific to the parts of the body that need preservation. Their sounds are harsh and guttural, seldom uttered by civilized tongues. The invalid must memorize dozens of them in order to be prepared, at any moment, to fight the corruptions that might advance on his flesh.

But while the inheritance of these hymns from the sorcerers of old is an astonishing stroke of fortune, they too have their limitations. *Tabes arcana* can affect the organs of thought and memory, and in such cases even seasoned practitioners can seldom coax the appropriate hymn from the mumbling lips of the invalid. Nothing can stop the disease then, and piece by piece it consumes its victim.

Many thinkers have offered conjectures about the origin of the hymns. Some warn that they may be chants to pagan gods, while others claim that, to possess such power, they must be written in the language through which the One True God animates all Creation. Since no earthly language bears any resemblance to that of the hymns, this debate may never be settled.

It stands to reason that if recitations can relieve the throes of *Tabes arcana*, they may even be able to cure it. Scholars hypothesize that an unknown hymn exists which would permanently dispel the humors of the disease. Some scholars carry this reasoning further and conjecture that there must also be hymns with the capacity to heal other infirmities, perhaps even lengthen life beyond its natural span. A theoretician recently strung the syllables together in a new, untried fashion, hoping to stumble upon a formula for immortality. But the treachery of the hymns soon became apparent. The syllables could harm as well as heal, and he lost both limb and life.

Insania communalis

Once a contagion resembling *Insania communalis* has been reported, the authorities quarantine the town to contain the evil humors. The isolated town then descends into chaos and filth, and months of suffering pass before the gates can be opened and order restored.

Insania communalis severs the link between cause and effect. One person's inability to find food lights an urgent hunger in another, which causes a third to consume stale meat, upsetting the guts of a fourth. An upright citizen violates an innocent, in order to quench the lust of a stranger. The guilt of the crime then torments a third person, inciting a fourth to slit his wrists, followed by yet another's death from hemorrhage. The effect also ripples in the other direction. A woman unrelated to the victim finds herself pregnant, while yet another bears the shame of being despoiled. Such fragmentation of desire and thought, of thought and action, of action and consequence causes the town to degenerate into a den of lunatics. They can only stagger and lurch, stripped of all purpose.

Insania communalis is a misnomer. Practitioners named it at a time when there was no way to distinguish it from other kinds of contagious insanity. The diagnosis is still difficult to make, as physicians dare not visit the town until the last traces of the disease have gone. Then they question the inhabitants, urging them to recall everything that happened during the days of contagion. Based on these testimonies, the physicians try to identify the splinters of events which should have involved a single person, but which, as a result of the disease, span the lives of a dozen or more. Only physicians with decades of expertise can detect the telltale splintering of *Insania communalis,* for the recollections are every bit as disordered as the town itself. One man may have committed a crime, while another remembers it.

The period of contagion is therefore one of moral chaos, in which the traditional scales of sin and virtue are useless. A recent treatise claims that the knots of cause and effect are so tangled that not even an omniscient being could tell who bears the fault for which action. This treatise has been condemned, and rightly so. It carries within it the seeds of a blasphemous argument: that even God can be forced into suspending His judgments, and that by a contagion of His own making.

Osteitis deformans preciosa

The invalid with *Osteitis deformans preciosa* first notices curvatures in his phalangeal bones. Over the next few weeks, his fingers curl backwards until the nails are flat against the back of his hands. The toes likewise fold back onto the dorsum of his foot. The condition is painless thus far, but the changes are so terrifying that the invalid brings himself to the attention of a physician.

Unfortunately, no treatment can stop the progression of *Osteitis deformans preciosa*. The bones of the wrists fold back over the forearms, which themselves curl towards the elbows. The shins bend until ankles press against knees. Then the large bones themselves deform and coil back, and the invalid is reduced to a head and torso with grotesque rolls for limbs.

The vertebrae then twist, bowing the invalid's pelvis to his sternum, while the ribs tighten like vises around his chest. The invalid's torment ceases to be a matter of mere dread. Unbearable pain and suffocation set in. The last moments are gruesome, for the invalid and for all witnesses, and physicians administer opium in liberal quantities to ease the passage.

But the disease doesn't stop at death. Indeed, it quickens. Funeral rites have to be performed in haste, for the skull crumples and the shoulders collapse before the eyes of the mourners, who hurry to consign what remains of the body to the earth. The family of the invalid, or else some wealthy patron whom the physician has alerted to an opportunity for profit, appoints armed guards at the cemetery to keep the grave from being plundered.

A year later, the coffin is exhumed. The flesh has all been eaten away by worms and insects, and sometimes clumps of hair are found in the coffin, along with nails and teeth that rattle like pebbles. But the bones themselves have been crushed into a thing of ferocious beauty. A spherical diamond the size of an eyeball, perfect in its clarity and internal symmetry, is all that remains of the invalid's skeleton.

Scholars have offered no mechanism to explain *Osteitis deformans preciosa*. The disease has spurred speculations on the origins of gemstones found in mountains and mineshafts—what species of burrowing creatures might have had the right bones to produce each one? But the diamonds of *Osteitis deformans preciosa* are different in one crucial way. Though their quality is such that they can sell at ten times the price of others their size, the purchase comes with a risk. In one of every ten cases, the affliction will release the invalid from its grip many decades after death. An incident involving a duchess of Burgundy put a swift end to the fashion of wearing these diamonds as jewelry. She was found in her chamber, her face white and bloodless, her heart stopped by shock. A full skeleton lay draped across her chest where the diamond had once hung, in an ornate setting fashioned after the Byzantine style.

Confusio linguarum

After a plague of *Confusio linguarum* has swept a town, its squares and brothels, its churches and abattoirs all fill with citizens lamenting in tongues never before uttered on this earth. The victims never recover their native languages and can only speak thereafter in strange new syllables.

Once the epidemic is no longer contagious, brave linguists enter the city, hoping to decipher the vocabularies and grammars that the infestation has left behind. They act as healers, wrenching meaning from desperate, cryptic babbling. But the task of translating languages that have never before existed is arduous, and few linguists can perform it with any skill. The ones who can are susceptible, like all men, to the lure of gold and offer their services primarily to the rich. The languages of merchants are always the first to be unraveled. Dry conversations about trade and governance begin, while the words of poets and philosophers go unheard. But one mustn't criticize the linguists too harshly. They provide their services at great risk. More than one linguist, trapped in a relapse of the epidemic, lost his mastery of ancient and modern languages and was cursed to live with a single invented one.

Most of the townsfolk, for lack of an interpreter, are left to their own devices. It is common to see public monuments defaced by words scribbled in thousands of alphabets. Each scribbler is seeking companions granted a similar dialect with whom they might speak a single honest sentence. Some succeed, and they leave the blood relatives made distant by the disease. They embrace instead the mothers and brothers and lovers allotted to them by the vagaries of an epidemic, with whom they now hope to share intimacies in a tongue without history or heritage.

Conscientia errans

Many diseases can unravel the fragile tapestry of consciousness. It is not uncommon to see even robust men reduced to catatonia by overwhelming illnesses. Some return to health when their disorders are diagnosed and corrected, while for others, only the passage of time offers any hope for the turbulent humors to settle. *Conscientia errans*, or Wandering Consciousness, falls within the latter category, though its mechanisms are quite distinct from those of its neighbors.

Luck plays a major role in the diagnosis. Physicians, often during symposia at the Central Library, discuss their work with other practitioners and notice connections between invalids in their care. Diagnosis is easy to establish once the disease is suspected, for it takes only a few weeks of documentation to confirm the telltale pattern of *Conscientia errans*. Each group consists of no more than five invalids, only one of whom is granted wakefulness at a given time. When consciousness departs the body of one, leaving him insensate, it passes to another. Taken individually, the invalids appear merely to lapse in and out of awareness, but the coordination of the episodes of inertia and arousal is so flawless that it argues in favor of an unbroken ribbon running through them all. The memories and personalities of the invalids are unchanged, and the disease makes no attempt to erode their distinctive features. They remain unaware of each other's existence, but on rare occasions the memories of one might bleed into another, so that an invalid might have a detailed dream of an unfamiliar town, or recollect lines from a play he has never watched.

Many hypotheses have been advanced to explain this affliction. One theory rejects the idea of a single itinerant consciousness and argues that the invalids suffer from a pathology whose waxing and waning works like the cascading illumination of fireflies, thus producing the mere illusion of migration. A second theory argues that the original souls of all these invalids have been devoured and replaced by a single parasitic soul, which abandons its habitual wanderings outside the world of men and cloaks itself in their bodies for a time. While the actions of the invalids might appear to be autonomous, the will of the parasite governs everything they do. A third theory argues, more provocatively, that the disease is a conspiracy by the invalids to defy mortality. They are slated in the divine ledgers for imminent death, but their souls, in repudiation of that judgment, prolong themselves by rationing the meager quantities of consciousness left to them.

Amnesia histrionis

Grand doyens of the stage are struck with terror at the very mention of *Amnesia histrionis*, for they have all known peers crippled by the illness. They whisper of veteran actors who, seated before their mirrors with painted faces, realized in the moments before the raising of the curtain that every line they had ever memorized was slipping away from them. They wrung their hands in anguish, trying desperately to resurrect Oedipus and Antigone or to rekindle the torment of Phaedra, the pride of Agamemnon, the grief of Demeter. The decaying flowers of past glory surrounded them, but their mirrors reflected mere imposters, dressed as emperors or philosophers or demigods in the dull yellow light of the candles.

The disease spares all memories unrelated to the theater and leaves all other faculties untouched. Those with *Amnesia histrionis* remain fully aware of the magnitude of their loss and remember the adulation once showered upon them. Unable to commit dialogue to memory, many abandon the arts altogether and recede into the corners of seedy taverns, the usual chronology of their careers reversed. But there are some who only turn their backs on the world of scripted theater and enter instead the world of improvisation. The disease does not harm their ability to shape characters and craft narrative lines, and they draw from their imaginations performances of great complexity and depth, knowing that they will neither be able to repeat the ones that bring them acclaim nor refine the ones that are criticized.

No thespian afflicted with *Amnesia histrionis* has ever been known to recover, and though most are robbed of their livelihood and stature, they are also granted an unexpected gift. The plays on their bookcases are changed from old friends to seductive strangers, and each page offers pleasures they would otherwise never have known on a second reading.

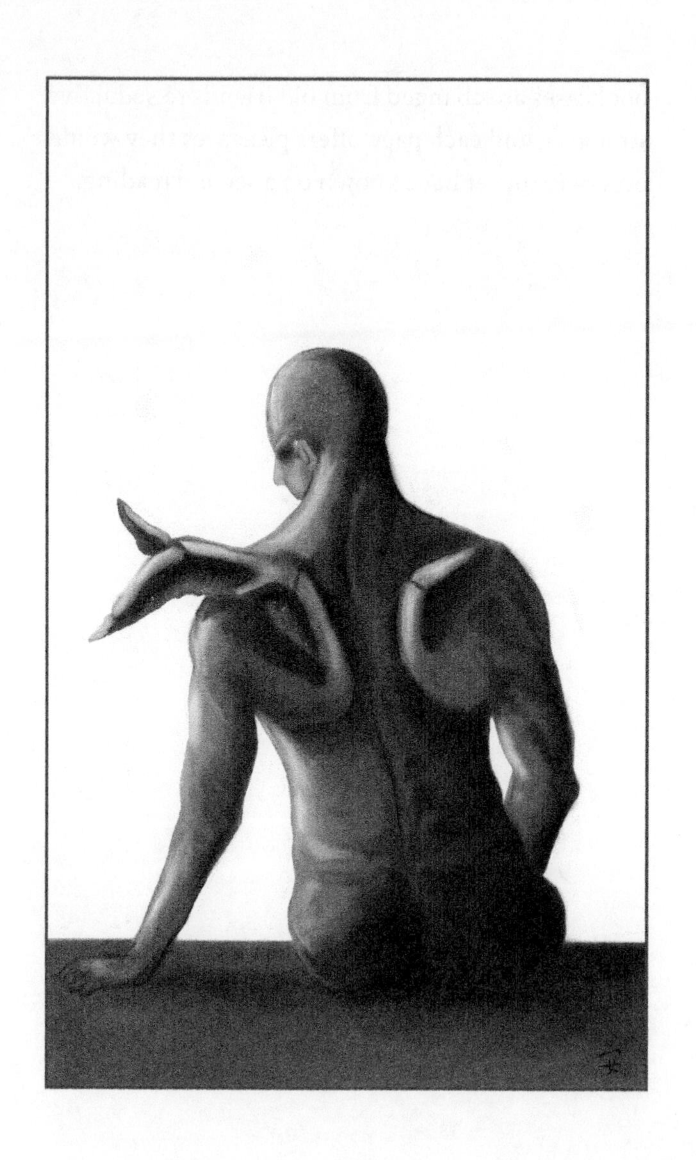

Membrum vestigiale

Some say *Membrum vestigiale,* or Vestigial Limb, is a misnomer, but the nomenclature has persisted because it describes the most obvious feature of the disease: a limb bud, which typically sprouts from the scapula. The bud is first identified at birth and grows until adolescence, when it may reach the length of a forearm.

It is not uncommon for extra fingers and toes to branch from the limbs of otherwise healthy people, and such extra digits rarely cause the person any harm. But in *Membrum vestigiale,* not only is the extra appendage bigger, it is almost never the only abnormality present. The afflicted also suffer webbed toes, double rows of teeth, redundant chambers in the heart. Some of these defects are externally evident, others are detectable only on necropsy. Certain theoreticians suggest that the condition results from the same processes that create grotesque infants with multiple heads and arms and interlocked spines, but many within the medical fraternity disagree, believing there is more to these vestigial limbs.

A compelling anatomical treatise argues that the buds sprouting from the scapulae have little in common with human arms and instead contain bones as hollow as those in avian wings. Another report describes how the soft coatings of these buds are reminiscent of primordial feathers. Some have found dormant claws in the invalids' fingers, while others have noted the shedding of their skins.

Membrum vestigiale is perhaps a disease of truncated ambition, a sign of some yearning within man to escape the limits nature places on him. Our crude tools allow us to document only the defects visible to the eye, but there may well be others that are hidden to us. One can only speculate as to their nature: primordial tissues with the potential to confer clairvoyance, glands capable of secreting patience and perseverance, perhaps even outgrowths from the fragile organ of compassion, resistant to the atrophy that so rapidly consumes its natural counterpart.

Continued reports of *Membrum vestigiale*, coupled with its failure to produce a single fully formed organ that would elevate the afflicted one above the common condition of mankind, demonstrate that God is swift to censor creatures that aspire to abilities they do not yet deserve to possess.

Seasonal Paralysis

In monsoon-battered lands the first downpour infects whole villages, and they fall into a strange stillness. For two days and two nights the bow of the violinist hangs above his strings, the clay of the potter dries out and crumbles in his hands, the quill of the author drips dark blotches on his paper. The lips of the babe stay clamped around the teat, the needle of the seamstress rests against her thumb, the fingers of the adolescent grip his member. Those whose eyes were closed are imprisoned behind their eyelids. The others must stare, for two days and two nights, at the scene before them.

Throughout the course of this illness, the minds of the invalids remain alert to the full horror of their paralysis. The heavy rains go on. Curtains of water pound those unfortunate enough to be caught standing outside, while those kneeling before a fire are scorched. Lovers trapped in each other's arms must fight against a furiously rising despair, as the union that began with lust now sours into a terrible agony, while their faces remain stamped with the contortions of their pleasure. The cuckold who happened to walk in on a scene of adultery cannot turn away from the ruins of his happiness, from this portrait of two bodies that have no need for a third.

Only the rarest persons escape the clutch of Seasonal Paralysis. They are free to walk around and observe, as if through the eyes of God, scenes of kindness and cruelty that would otherwise have passed unseen. They wonder why they were spared, whether their families will ever be restored, or whether they are now the keepers of an eternal menagerie of sculptures. They witness frozen lives that will soon be forever altered, for when the paralysis lifts, the invalids cease to be the people they were before. They cannot return to their old selves, not after their time as effigies in stone.

The germ of Seasonal Paralysis has not been identified. By the time the healers of the land thaw from their own petrifaction, the rains are benign again. The water bears only life and rejuvenation, and the more ordinary diseases of the monsoon season.

IV.

Oh, yes, the madman, you want to know about him? Ricardo Mateus was a scholar himself. He was young but had already written ten or fifteen treatises and would spend hours in this hall, poring through the *Encyclopaedia* and looking for ways to refine his own work. A respected man.

And then, one day, he smuggled in a tinderbox. A small thing, hidden in his robes. He settled on one of these benches—that one, in fact, three rows over—and pretended to be engrossed in study. Except that he was striking the flint without drawing attention to himself. He managed to get a small fire started, a paper flame, and poured enough oil on the table to get the wood smoking. Some librarians—we didn't have guards at the time—tackled him and managed to wrest the *Encyclopaedia* volume from his grip before he could scorch it. Apart from some damage to the binding, which we replaced, the pages themselves were unharmed, God be praised. Parchment doesn't burn easily. But ever since that day, the Library, and especially this hall, has had royal guards.

The king's soldiers tortured Ricardo, of course. They say he raved about the *Encyclopaedia* being an abomination before God, a work of hubris that couldn't be allowed to stand. Then one of the torturers twisted a screw with a little too much enthusiasm, and the testimony ended.

Ricardo was an odd character—affable one moment, moody the next. He threw a tantrum in public when a scholar he loathed deposited a treatise in this Library on a topic he'd been studying. For a year before the incident, he'd become obsessed with disorders of memory. His colleagues had noticed his behavior growing stranger during that time. He would refuse to speak to anyone in the dining hall, or he would lock himself in his room and scribble away into the night. I read through his writings after his death. They were recollections of his childhood and the home in which he was raised. Meticulous accounts of the rooms, the courtyard, the people in his life. He devoted fifty pages to his mother, another fifty to a girl he had loved in his youth.

You see the blackened corner of this desk? That's the spot where he tried to get the wood burning. We decided not to replace the teak. It's good to remember such things.

Mirrored Amnesia

The invalid with *Amnesia esoptrica,* or Mirrored Amnesia, when still in the prime of his life, begins to notice blank spots in his memory. When he thinks of the interior of his village chapel, he can no longer picture the crucifix that ought to hang there. He cannot recall the names or faces of the boys who sang with him in the village choir. He can forge horseshoes but has no recollection of ever having entered a smithy. He recalls once fleeing from an orchard with an apple clutched in his hand but cannot remember climbing the tree to pluck it.

He remembers a round breast with a tiny scar, glorious in its imperfection, but not the identity of the woman who possessed it, or how he became privy to such an intimate detail.

Day after day he combs the corridors of his mind and finds yet more things missing, and begs his friends and relatives to help him illuminate the voids. They recount their secondhand recollections of his life, until he knows his own history mostly by hearsay. It is in this absurd fashion that he must live, for only by memorizing the fragmented recollections of others can he hope to have any semblance of a past.

But the affliction overtakes his efforts at compensation. He begins to lose the part of himself that was known to him alone, witnessed by no other. He is left with no recourse but to fill his mind with suppositions and conjectures, with imagined memories of music he might have heard, lovers he might have wooed, sins he might have committed.

Scholars of memory report that in the terminal stages of *Amnesia esoptrica,* when all of the invalid's own memories have been erased, he forgets even his own diseased state. He possesses only the fictions he has created in an attempt to bandage his failing mind and repeats them, again and again, as though they were truth. He wanders as a minstrel or a madman, for depending on the nature of the tales he has woven for himself, his fellow men regard him as a great storyteller—or a moonstruck fool.

Corpus fractum

The symptoms of *Corpus fractum* are unique in each case. An affluent young woman of Norse descent was diagnosed with *Corpus fractum* when she woke up, to her great alarm, with the olive skin and strong jaw of the Mediterranean governess who had cared for her decades ago, then died in penury. An aging knight was distressed when his eyebrows grew thick and bushy like those of the farmer he'd lanced in a drunken rage. A priest grew frantic when his lips turned plump like those of the girl with whom he'd spent a night of sin and then driven out of town when her belly began to swell.

The disease is seldom restricted to just a single transformation, and in severe cases the invalid becomes a patchwork: he has the aquiline nose of the patron he betrayed, the low ears of the friend whose gold he stole, the fleshy jowl of the grandmother he neglected, the balding forehead of the penniless tenant he threw out on the streets. The condition is not disfiguring, any more than the natural variation of the human race is a source of disfigurement. For every maiden whose shapely nose is replaced by a crooked one, there is another who receives arched eyebrows and high cheekbones.

Some theologians argue that *Corpus fractum* is not a disease at all. Repentance is a bitter draught, they say, and most men refuse to drink it. *Corpus fractum*, by plastering their sins on their faces, forces them to confront their pasts every time they glance into a mirror. In that respect it is a remedy, not an affliction.

Oraculum terribile

Among the inmates of our madhouses are found occasional invalids with *Oraculum terribile,* a condition often mistaken for insanity. It strikes its victims in the fourth decade of their lives, and they begin to rave like madmen. In solitude their faces are blank, but the moment another human being enters their presence, they scream and flail and squeeze their palms over their eyelids in a frantic effort to shut out sights only they can see, all the while blabbering about torture and flagellation and visions of hellfire that they describe in horrific detail.

The nature of this disease was first illuminated in a treatise that shook the medical fraternity. Invalids with *Oraculum terribile,* though unacquainted with one another and separated by great distances, reacted in exactly the same way to the presence of the same visitor. This observation had escaped the authorities for centuries, for the disease is uncommon and its sufferers far separated. A few brave scholars traveled from asylum to asylum, faced every invalid they could find, and documented the horrible words they spoke. Their accounts demonstrated that all the invalids were unanimous, as though they had conspired with each other, in their verdicts on the precise torment that every visitor would suffer in the afterlife.

Once this was reported, the whole world shunned these invalids, for no one, either within the medical establishment or without, had the courage to confront visions of such violent portent about their own souls. The stewards of asylums began to place the invalids under solitary custody, arguing that solitude afforded the invalids calm lives, free of the visions that would otherwise torture them.

No consensus has been reached about the implications of the malady for the collective fate of the human race. The chaos is understandable, for the alternatives are equally repugnant: that the disease is a capricious and sadistic farce perpetrated by God, or that all humanity is, without exception, condemned to eternal damnation.

Dictio aliena

Dictio aliena is often dismissed as a trifling inconvenience. It is common to hear of its sufferers being turned away from the doors of apothecaries in favor of those whose pains require urgent care. But the intimate friends of the disease's victims can attest to the depth of their loneliness, for the illness estranges them from the society of their brethren.

Farmers and blacksmiths struck with *Dictio aliena* awaken on their humble straw beds with the speech and inflections of aristocrats. Their consonants are crisp, their vowels haughty, their delivery florid. Squatting around bonfires with their simple, baffled neighbors, they speak with excruciating politeness and, unbeknownst to them, pretension. Barons and dukes experience the opposite trauma. Their cultivated diction degenerates into the frank, coarse speech of townsfolk and laborers, with garbled syntax and words devoid of culture and breeding. In the span of a single night, the speech of the invalids transforms beyond recognition, and even though their language remains intelligible, their friends and families no longer feel a sense of kinship towards them, for every word they utter bears the stamp of a culture entirely alien to their own.

The treatment of *Dictio aliena* is prolonged and painstaking, for it requires sufferers to relearn a manner of speech that was once second nature to them. Even after they wean themselves from the habits of the disease, and their communities are able to welcome them once again, they harbor a deep sense of alienation. There are members of the nobility whose squires hear them moan and curse each night in the earthy voices of village men, giving vent in their souls to the only voices they feel to be truly their own, voices they now must silence in the company of their equals.

So great are the tortures of *Dictio aliena* that an Earl of Warwick abandoned his rank and claim to the English throne when he realized he could never be fully cured. He wandered for months as a minstrel until he came upon a hamlet whose inhabitants spoke like he did. He lived in that village till the end of his days, sleeping on its coarse mats, eating its frugal meals, speaking its humble dialect.

Pestis divisionis

Visitors to the Central Library often bring tales of lands devastated by *Pestis divisionis.* In the days before this plague strikes, the mutilated corpses of rats begin to surface in sewers and alleys. People bundle their possessions and try to flee, hoping to escape the ravages of the disease.

But before many can leave, *Pestis divisionis* erupts across the land. The victims find their loyalties dissolved and replaced by new allegiances. They form sects whose differences are so deep and acrimonious that every person abandons his home to join his new brothers. The differences are never traceable to race or religion or ancestry: they are mere fictions imposed by the plague.

Soon after, the bloodshed begins, as the new clans battle over soil they once shared in peace. Neighbors who used to tend each other's farms now chop each other with scythes. Men crush their brothers' throats, while women stir poison into their children's milk. They are fully aware of the bonds they once shared, but they cannot imagine how they ever loved such vile insects.

Once the plague passes, the citizens witness the devastation of their own making through eyes no longer clouded by *Pestis divisionis*. Now come the killings of revenge, killings of grief, killings of madness, killings that hope to set right the killings committed during the plague. This is the true horror of *Pestis*: that its scars never leave the town. Bloodshed continues for generations after the disease has run its course.

Unable to cure the plague, apothecaries have made potions to reduce its misery. Invalids who drink them can quell the hatreds that haunt them. It takes many doses, many months of treatment, but finally they cut every thread that bound them to home and family. They leave the cursed town, turn into wanderers with new names and identities, and are free of the disease. Memories of the plague, and of those they have left behind, still come to them in nightmares—but when they wake they drink another draught of the potion, which they always keep at their bedside.

Napoli's Disease

Napoli's Disease might be considered a blessing if not for the fact that it infects precisely the people least able to cope with its effects. Scholars have suggested that the affliction may be the severest form of what is really a common ailment, so that those who receive a formal diagnosis are merely its most extreme victims.

Sufferers of Napoli's Disease develop soaring fevers that no nostrum or balm can control. Their eyes roll into their skulls and seizures wrack them. They remain that way for days, unable to eat or drink, unresponsive to the world. Then, when death seems near, the acute episode resolves and the invalids awaken, their bodies free of inflammation. They speak of visions granted to them, revelations of symmetry and perfection that they struggle to describe. Obsessed with these visions, they try to pour them out through every possible medium. But lacking the genius of great artists and composers, they flounder. Their faltering brushstrokes, their clumsy polyphony, their stilted sculptures drive them to despair. Still driven, they churn out works of ever-greater mediocrity. Aware of the chasm between their intent and their creations, they neglect their work, their families, and their health, and recede into darkness and torment.

The Central Library holds the works of one such invalid, bequeathed to the Library by his widow. Two dusty halls, seldom opened to the public, contain the entire output of his diseased years: nine hundred paintings, seventy-eight figurines, forty-five books, two hundred poems, and thirty-three cantatas. A sense of tragic ambition fills these works. The invalid toiled until his fingers bled and his eyes grew dim, but none of his works show any sign of greatness. Taken alone, each work possesses barely a trace of the original inspiration. But taken together, these malformed embryos may contain, fragmented between them, the totality of the vision that drove him. Visitors try to identify these fragments—a brushstroke here, a musical motif there—and piece them together until a single work, perhaps one of genius, can emerge from the vast expanse of mediocrity. They have made little progress. If there is a masterpiece there, it must transcend any physical medium. Never intended for this world, perhaps it can exist only in the fevered mind.

Virginitas aeterna

Virginitas aeterna, a disease lamented as bitterly by the husbands of those afflicted with it as by the women themselves, illustrates the trouble with overzealous healing mechanisms, for the invalid's body insists on repairing, and restoring to pristine condition, parts of the anatomy that are best left damaged.

The hymen in women with this condition, whether ruptured by surgery or fornication, persistently mends itself, and neither excision nor scarification produces lasting relief. Due to the repeated restoration of maidenhood, every sexual congress brings the pain and anxiety of a fresh deflowering. Most women with this condition develop a keen aversion to all sensuality. There are some who brave the discomfort with the goal of motherhood in mind, but even this is not without risk: there have been cases of prolonged, arduous labor, in which slits had to be made in the hymen every few minutes to counteract the continuous repair. There was even the unfortunate case of a girl who was found at adolescence to have a hymen without perforation, a condition normally cured by a simple fenestration. The membrane persisted in sealing itself into an impermeable wall, damming in her menstrual flow every month. Only with surgical perforation twice a day during the period of her menses was she able to survive.

As if the torments of this condition were not enough, profiteers are always waiting to exploit the invalids. Nothing is more valuable to a brothel owner than a girl with *Virginitas aeterna*. Rich men, inflamed by scripture and folklore into a thirst for the purity of virgins, will travel for miles to claim the innocence of a maiden. Once the deed is done, they leave, their lust sated, unaware that these maidens have known many men, and that their innocence has been fractured beyond repair, for they have known blood and pain far more often than they have known the tenderness that ought to temper it.

Chorea rhythmica

Disorders of movement are common, but *Chorea rhythmica* is no ordinary disease. An episode usually begins with debilitating muscle spasms. The invalid's limbs flail of their own will, their wrists contort at strange angles, their arms toss in the air. Left untreated, the disease progresses to the shoulders and thighs and torso, until the invalid is left with no volition. Thus the disease is often confused with demonic possession, an entirely different sort of affliction.

In the absence of a diagnosis, the invalid suffers terribly for weeks before dying of starvation. Only the astute physician recognizes the rhythm and cadence of *Chorea rhythmica*. He observes the flailing invalid and identifies patterns within the motions. Using complex equations, he calculates the proportions of tinctures needed to produce a remission. In concert with the movements, he and his apprentices administer them: two drops of elecampane each time the neck snaps back, a sprinkle of ground mandragora when an elbow extends, a grain of black salt at the clenching of the fists. The disease falls back, and except for a slight tremor, the invalid regains control of his body. But the treatment doesn't cure the disease, and when it recurs the physician needs to calculate new proportions and sequences of tinctures to control it.

Some theoreticians believe that the healing power of these tinctures lies not in the ingredients, but in the rhythm and pattern of their administration. One scholar suggests that physicians would do better to replace them with sound, produced at the bedside by musicians trained in disorders of movement. At every spasm of *Chorea rhythmica*, they would play musical lines in sharp counterpoint. With this they could respond to the movements more efficiently than with a sequence of tinctures.

At least one report describes an invalid who, struck by the promise of this treatment, undertook a rigorous education in counterpoint and harmony. Now, at the first hint of *Chorea,* he hums a counter-theme of such precision that the spasms never progress beyond a mild twitching.

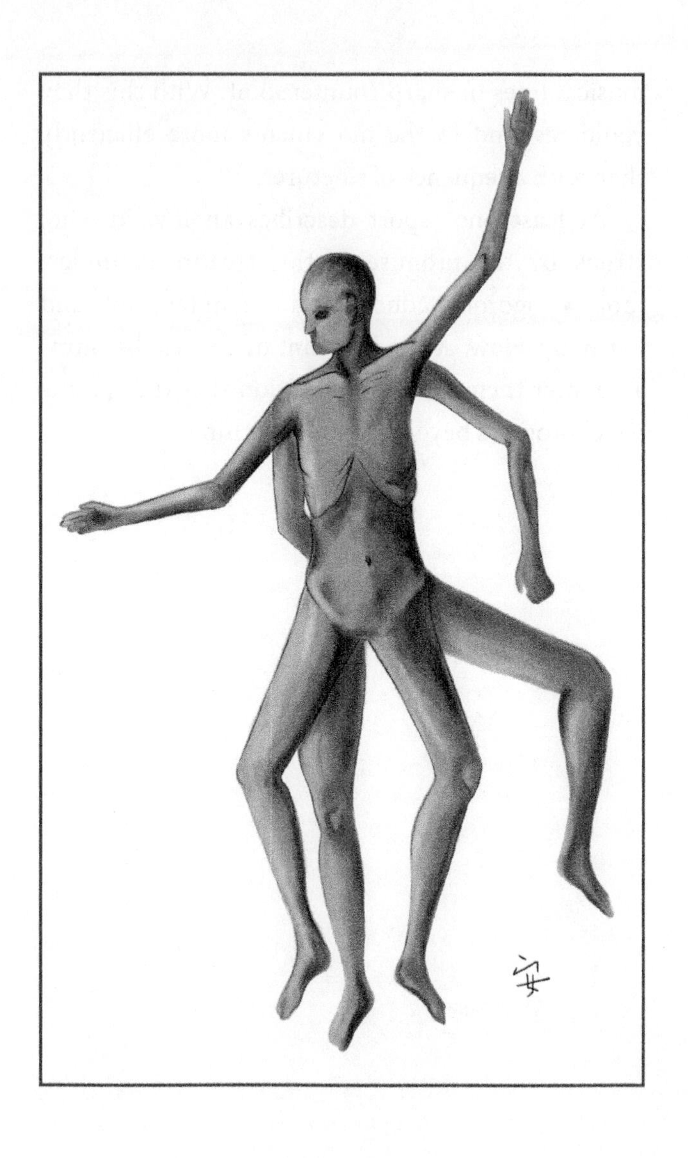

V.

We've been drifting aimlessly from volume to volume here, Máximo, which was my intention—I just wanted to give you a taste of the *Encyclopaedia* and its contents. Some day, you should consider reading it from beginning to end. It's an illuminating experience. The *Encyclopaedia* is organized in a careful hierarchy. The first level is based on anatomy, the next on pathological mechanisms, and further branches on minutiae concerning each particular class of afflictions.

The branches grow ever finer, until maladies listed on adjacent pages differ from each other only in their subtlest nuances. If you read the *Encyclopaedia* from beginning to end, you get the feeling that every affliction known to man is part of a single, infinite progression. Or that every disease is a different facet of one great and terrible malady.

Pay attention to these things, Máximo, as you begin your apprenticeship here. Try to understand the structure of the Library, not just memorize its categories. That can make the difference between a great librarian and a merely competent one.

Hypersomnia fatalis

Suspicions of *Hypersomnia fatalis* arise when incurable insomniacs are suddenly blessed with nights of deep, unbroken sleep. The rest relieves their fatigue, the dark circles under their eyes vanish, and their stooped backs straighten. They abandon the taverns where they drank Morphean brews in a miserable search for oblivion, the alleys where they pined for lost loves, the morbid lamps under which they counted the cobblestones in the pavement. They return to the beds that once witnessed their torment, and the creaks that used to keep them awake now lull them to sleep.

In their dreams they conjure an exact replica of the world they inhabited while awake. Well-rested and jovial, they visit its cheerful taverns and toast the health of their compatriots, stroll its grand promenades and seduce new lovers, sit under the soft moonlight and count the twinkling stars. In the domain of sleep they enjoy, in full measure, all the pleasures that eluded them in the world of wakefulness.

As *Hypersomnia fatalis* progresses, the need for this rejuvenating sleep extends beyond the hours of night. As morning approaches and the invalids come to the end of their jaunts through the dream world, they imagine that they lay their heads on pillows to go to sleep, only to awake in the world of daylight, a capricious and arbitrary province. They look forward to escaping it, that they might enter once again the gentler realm of night. They pass through months of expanding nights and shrinking days, until at last the days shrink to nothingness, and they remain forever immersed in sleep. Soon thereafter, their bodies, groomed to perfection in the domain of darkness but untended in the domain of light, cease all functioning.

A group of renegade somnologists argue that the term *Hypersomnia fatalis* is a misnomer. The invalids are still insomniacs, but insomniacs who have transitioned from a world that denied them sleep to one in which they have no further need of it. They are awake in the dream world and content to live there, and they feel no desire to fall asleep and awaken into the nightmare of day. These somnologists decry the use of the suffix *fatalis*. "It is arrogant," they write, "that we deny their domain of dreams the privileges we grant to our own domain of wakefulness. We, who walk in the light of day, would not consider someone to have died if he were to expire in a dream. Why must the same courtesy not be extended to the dreamers?"

Empathia pathologica

Empathia pathologica is perhaps best known for the cults that have arisen among its sufferers, though the vast majority of the invalids lead inconspicuous lives. The ledgers in the Central Library that document cases of this disease have grown much thicker in recent years, and while it is possible that the prevalence of the disease is on the rise, it is far more likely that physicians have gotten better at diagnosing it and have stopped confusing it with other, more mundane, disorders of emotion.

Individuals with *Empathia pathologica* develop a crippling susceptibility to the moods of others. Their emotional states swing dramatically under the influence of people in their company. Large crowds provoke the greatest distress, forcing invalids to cycle through a gamut of emotions, but in smaller groups they can learn to exercise some control, suppressing the flow of emotions from some people and modulating what comes from others. With experience they develop the ability to focus their diseased empathy with skill and accuracy. They are never able to rid themselves entirely of undesired intrusion, however. It is only in absolute seclusion, far from all human contact, that those with *Empathia pathologica* can be certain they are savoring joys or sorrows that are truly their own.

The cults that form among these invalids have been written of widely and condemned by the Church. Adolescents fresh from the chaos of their tormented worlds, youths weary of the turmoil within their peers, elderly invalids fatigued by the lifelong stigma of mental infirmity, are all drawn to these cults. They shun the company of ordinary mortals and band together with others of their kind, in remote caves or abandoned crypts. There they cautiously drop their barriers and open their minds. Although early attempts are usually brought to agonizing failure by a stray fearful thought magnified within the echo chamber of their minds, with experience they can titrate the flow of emotion. Then, in moments of perfect synchrony, their resonating minds taste heights of ecstasy that far surpass any sane pleasure.

These pleasures are sometimes of the basest physical kind, which must be condemned for their immodesty if nothing else. But some cults take more troubling paths. They claim that they seek only the rarefied pleasures of the mind and that their disease grants them experiences of radiant bliss. But this bliss always leads them to believe that the disease has liberated them from a cycle of birth and death in which their souls were trapped since the beginning of time. Cults based in different lands, whose members have had no contact with each other, all receive the same heresy from *Empathia pathologica*. To stem this tide, the Church has banned the congregation of more than two invalids with *Empathia pathologica* at any place.

Glossolalia cryptica

Those afflicted with *Glossolalia cryptica* lose the ability to speak their native tongue at the first touch of the disease, producing instead strings of nonsensical, haphazard syllables. Their recitations bear however the rhythm and cadence of insightful speech, and theologians often claim that these invalids have received a gift from the divine Spirit.

Cryptographers poring through these recitations are able to identify encrypted anecdotes and fables and moral tales. But the fables themselves are ciphers. Shrewd interpreters manage to unriddle this next layer of encryption, pulling a profound dialectic from within the simple narratives. It has recently been discovered, however, that these arguments are themselves enciphered messages. Only a handful of living cryptographers can unravel them further.

A recent declaration from the Fellowship of Cryptographers states that their work so far has merely skimmed the surface of the utterances, and that beneath every new interpretation lies a deeper layer of revelations. The next ciphers are as impenetrable as granite. The cryptographers have combed through their textbooks and manuscripts and consulted the writings of Alberti and Polybius, of Trithemius and Al-Kindi, hoping to find clues to guide their path forward, but at present they find themselves stymied. They end their declaration with the conjecture that the final layer underlying the deepest ciphers may contain answers to eternal questions about the nature of God and the foundations of truth, answers whose pursuit is worthy of their unremitting toil. They do not, however, mention what is surely their greatest fear: that there may be no final revelation, but rather an endless regression of layers, each more opaque than the last.

It remains unclear whether individuals with *Glossolalia cryptica* are aware of the significance of their illness, for they make no attempt to unravel their own speech or translate their words into intelligible tongues. The disease grants them a strange serenity. They neglect the needs of their bodies and, little by little, waste away.

Torpor morum

When it reaches the peak of its severity, the paralysis that grips victims of *Torpor morum* can no longer be distinguished from that caused by a host of other afflictions. The milder forms of the illness, however, are easy to diagnose. Sufferers of *Torpor morum,* or Moral Paralysis, are incapable of recognizing gradations of morality. They feel a crippling obligation to contemplate in detail the adverse consequences of their actions. The forlorn faces of paupers or casual mentions of distant battles, which they once regarded with indifference, now assume grotesque, nauseating proportions. They are unable to tolerate the slightest suggestion of violence, even where dumb beasts are concerned. Meat and leather repulse them, and they grant animals absurd protections under the laws of their estates. Even ruthless hunters have been known to bury their crossbows and lances and destroy their collections of trophy heads after contracting the illness.

Those with *Torpor morum* make every attempt to speak the truth, but they cannot bear the ambiguities in even their truest statements and soon fall mute. Past this stage the disease is difficult to identify. In its most extreme form, when the turpitude inherent in the slightest movement becomes unbearable, paralysis sets in. The rare sufferers who have recovered report that only within the confines of pure thought were they able to draw solace from the abstract contemplation of virtue undiluted by vice.

In moral and philosophical circles the recognition of this illness has revived the eternal debate about the nature of the human conscience. There are none who deny that the conscience of man was crafted by God, who created man in His image. The disagreement among moralists lies in the hypotheses they advance to explain the disease. The traditionalists posit that *Torpor morum* is caused by a hypertrophy of the organ in which the conscience dwells, and that once this hidden organ has been identified, the definitive cure for the condition will be the surgical excision of the overgrown tissue. But the renegades ridicule this approach and propose instead a terrible and impious hypothesis. They argue that the insoluble problem of evil lies at the very crux of this disease. The injustices that riddle all existence must trouble God's own conscience, and if God indeed made man in His own image, He surely granted him not only a conscience but also the ability to suppress its voice at need. Just as the workings of heaven and earth would grind to a halt if God were unable to silence His divine conscience, the paralysis of *Torpor morum* is caused by the invalid's inability to silence his mortal conscience, the one faculty that, above all others, has allowed man dominion over the fish, the birds, the cattle, the earth.

Conceptus continuus

No treatise on *Conceptus continuus* yet graces the shelves of the Central Library, but we are likely to see one soon, for visiting scholars from India speak of the increasing prevalence of this disease in their land. Women with *Conceptus continuus* celebrate their exceptional fertility when the birth of their first child is followed closely by that of a second and a third. However, when the fourth, fifth, and sixth offspring are born in quick succession, the community's suspicions are raised. The disease has been known to cast aspersions

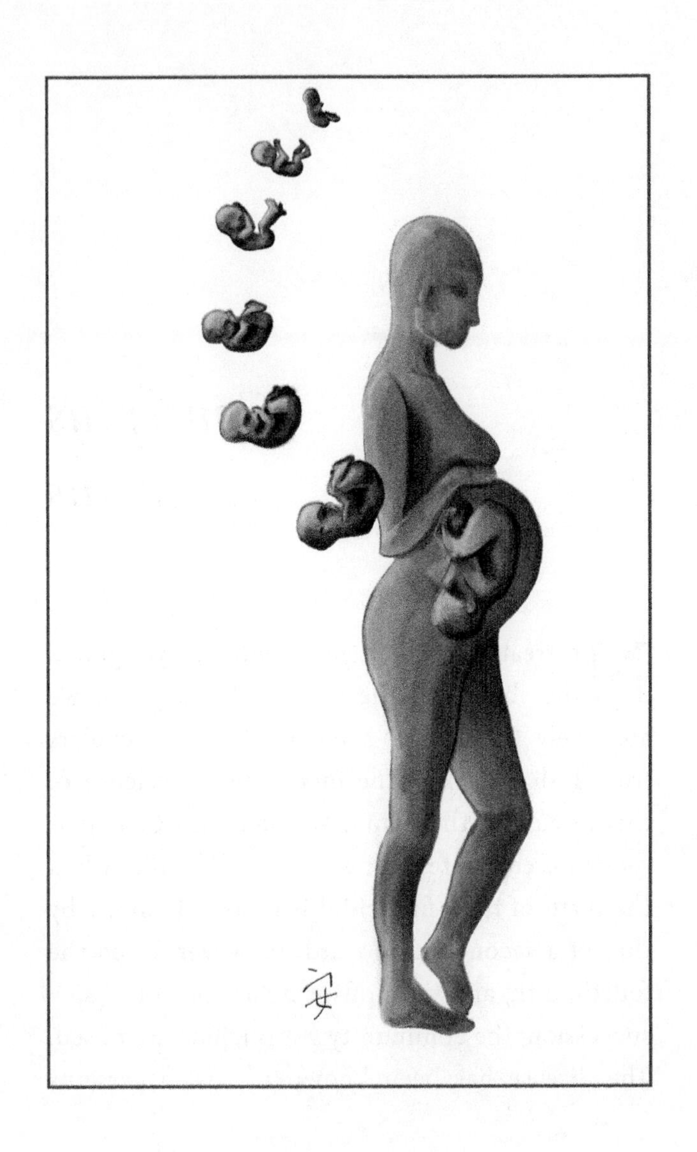
安

on the characters of innocent widows and women whose husbands are away at war. Men blind to its mechanisms accuse honest, loving wives of adultery.

The invalid with *Conceptus continuus* needs only be impregnated once, and then her womb is sentenced to a perpetually gravid state. Hardly is one infant born when another, a replica of the first, begins to develop—whether or not the woman experiences coitus ever again. Converted into little more than a vehicle for the passage of these infants, her strength is drained, and the exertions of gestation and birth confine her to her bed.

Added to the sufferings of this state is the discovery that each of the offspring is flawed. Some have deformities of the limbs, others of the heart, others of vision. Some appear to be spared, until they grow older and the devastating infirmities of their minds become apparent. Those who have had the opportunity to meet families resulting from this affliction describe the eerie sight of what appears to be a single individual captured simultaneously in every stage of its earthly growth, each with its own peculiar ailment, a progression of blemished variations on an unknown theme.

Because the disease is restricted to a handful of sufferers in a distant land, few of our own scholars have studied it. Those who have done so believe it occurs when the primordial essence of a single fetus is trapped within a malformed womb, and that the many progeny result from the repeated attempts of this trapped essence to escape its labyrinth. The visiting Indian scholars, however, diverge from this view. They believe that the disease represents a process of iteration, a futile attempt by nature to create the perfect human being. Most women with the malady eventually succumb to the physical toll exacted by endless birthing. The scholars theorize that, were these women to survive and continue indefinitely, the process would eventually culminate in the birth of a flawless infant devoid of imperfections, internal or external, a babe that would rival in form any that has ever been born. They refrain however from providing any estimate of how many iterations this process would take, or what the nature or import of this flawless infant would be.

But a third group of scholars present an entirely different hypothesis. They argue that if *Conceptus continuus* were a process of iteration, each of the offspring ought to be incrementally closer to perfection than the one that preceded it. The persistence of malformations, and the production of newer and crueler ones in each child, hints instead at a far more terrible mechanism. Perhaps this disease transforms the womb of the afflicted woman into a conduit between the mortal world and the divine agencies charged with voicing the displeasure of God, particularly the agencies to which the task of allotting deformities to unborn children has been entrusted.

Migratory Blindness

Our knowledge of this condition comes from the accounts of explorers and traders who have sailed to the frozen North. There is a certain tribe, they report, where one individual is always blind. He is termed the *qanuak,* or "unseeing one." According to the tribe's practices the *qanuak,* at the moment of blindness, becomes their most protected member, and the others attend to his every need. Perhaps the migratory nature of the blindness explains this privileged status, for every tribesman knows he might well be next.

Visiting merchants have never turned blind, so perhaps only members of this unfortunate tribe are susceptible to the affliction. But the fear of contagion has led neighboring peoples to lessen trade with them. Within the tribe itself contagiousness is a possible explanation for the disease, though an unsatisfying one, for after five lunar cycles the *qanuak* regains his vision and returns to normal life, while another person instantly becomes the *qanuak*.

Whether Migratory Blindness is myth or reality, it remains worthy of study. Three fables told in the tribe bear particular mention. The first is that of a foolish man who tried to rid the tribe of this blindness by stabbing the *qanuak* to death, only to find himself converted till the end of his days into the new *qanuak*. The second speaks of lovers bonded so deeply that when either of them turned into a *qanuak*, the other did as well. The third tells of a sorcerer who granted the gift of blindness to the tribe at the beginning of time, so that the suffering of a single man would atone for the sins of all. The *qanuak* would drink darkness, so others could drink light.

Dysacousis torrens

Many afflictions deprive their sufferers of hearing, but *Dysacousis torrens* is the only one that causes the greatest torment during the period of recovery. After a prolonged and stony deafness, people with this disease find their hearing restored in a most extraordinary manner. A floodgate opens and releases a torrent of sound, filling their minds with all the noise of the past. They hear the cascade of every rainfall they missed when they were deaf, the shattering groan of a thousand creaking doors, the mutiny of a million rustling autumn leaves.

It is after this piercing discord has died down that the voices begin. They hear the words they were never meant to hear: everything muttered in their presence during the time of deafness, insults shouted under the assumption that they would never reach the deadened ears, calumnies stored up with meticulous precision. They hear also the words of affection and annoyance that their lovers voiced: words spoken to the backs of their heads, longings whispered when their eyes were closed, revelations of the kind usually confided only to mirrors and gravestones. The curtain of deafness, once lifted, yields to a downpour of secrets.

On a shelf of the Central Library lie the records of the first known case of *Dysacousis torrens*. The invalid was a woman who regained her hearing after having been deprived of it for a decade. She was then subjected to the unrelenting voice of her now deceased husband, who for eight years had used her deaf ears in place of the latticed screen of the church confessional. "Forgive me, for I have sinned," his quivering voice had said to her as she cooked, as she spun, as she prayed. He poured out the tales of his infidelities to her unsuspecting back. Now, with her hearing restored, she learned that he had been frequenting brothels all those years. As his confessions continued, she felt first rage, then hatred, then grief. Finally, as the last of his bottled voice began to drain out, and she realized it was time for his second death, she forgave him.

Cursed Healer Syndrome

Cursed Healer Syndrome may be the disease that inspired the ideas of catharsis and lustration in pagan societies and led them to sacrifice animals in the hope that the transfer of evil humors from man to beast would cure maladies. Historical reports of this illness, though cloaked in parables, help confirm its persistence across civilizations. Almost every land has some tale of it.

The sufferer of Cursed Healer Syndrome, sometime in the fourth decade of his life, finds himself taking on the disfigurements of those around him.

People in his presence find the deviations in their noses corrected, the stains on their cheeks erased, the warts on their necks smoothed. While they are healed, the invalid transforms little by little into a ghoulish monstrosity. The knuckles of arthritic elders become slender as his own grow gnarled and twisted, the torsos of hunchbacks straighten as his spine arches and grows porous, the blind regain their vision as cataracts bloom in his eyes. The invalid tries to flee to forests and hilltops, far from all society, but the diseases of the nearest humans still find him. His fingers turn numb from leprosy, his brow grows fevered from the ague, his mind crumbles under premature senility. Sometimes he is captured and sold to wealthy lords, who force him to absorb the ills of their families. It takes little at this point to topple the invalid into the grave—a borrowed infection, an inherited palsy, a stranger's tumor.

Scholars believe that the seeds of this affliction lie in the purity of the healers' souls. Their empathy for the sick and decrepit is so great that it unweaves the threads of fate and transfers maladies from sufferer to healer. Guided by this premise, some physicians advocate a remedy that is as terrible as it is effective.

At the first hint of Cursed Healer Syndrome, they subject the invalid to an extensive indoctrination in misanthropy and conceit, training him to acquire from those around him not the blights of their bodies but the scars in their souls. By this method, invalids are able to suppress their curse and retain their health and vigor, but at an awful price. Their souls, once pure and vulnerable, are now converted into dank dungeons.

Theologians condemn this treatment. They point out that the age of onset of this disease is the same as the age at which the Redeemer was crucified. The disease may therefore be a gift from the Lord, an invitation to join Him in the cleansing of man's sinful nature. They urge invalids to suffer their disease in silence, and, through suffering, grow as close to the Lord as the greatest of saints.

At the first hint of Cursed Heart Syndrome, they [illegible]

[illegible] into dark dungeon.

[illegible]

VI.

I should have asked you when we began whether you believe those claims about consumption being contagious. Who knows what vapors I've been forcing on you all day? You don't believe that, do you? Good. Neither do I.

I just read an amusing treatise claiming that consumption is caused by a demonic dog gnawing the lungs of the invalid, causing him to spew blood and cough in a barking voice. Come to think of it, it's surprising how little I've coughed today. Perhaps my dog has found a bone.

The other night, I found myself wondering if there would be libraries in the afterlife. It's a silly thought, but, you see, my entire life has been devoted to this place. The *Encyclopaedia* is as familiar to me as my own body, and I've read every single one of these afflictions, but every time I read them I realize something new, a connection between afflictions in different volumes that I had never noticed before. It would be so pleasant to continue this in the beyond, to read and understand, and to think, most of all to think. The one fear I have about the afterlife is that all the connections among earthly things, people, and histories that I've spent my life puzzling out will look simple and obvious once I'm there. Every question will already have an answer. Nothing left to learn. That, for me, would not be heaven.

Don't look so astonished. The older I get, the freer I feel to wonder about such things. And don't worry about us being overheard. What are they going to do? Put an elderly librarian to the rack?

Lanfranco's Disease

Lanfranco's Disease was caused by the accidental detonation of gunpowder barrels at a small town carnival in Saxony. No one was killed, but the hundreds of carnivalgoers standing nearby were plunged into deafness. While the profundity of this deafness was remarkable even at the time, it was the future progress of the disease that would show its real peculiarities.

The ears of the invalids first started to ring, as is common in inflammations of the auditory apparatus. Physicians thought it was a sign that hearing would return, but never again did the invalids hear the sounds of the outside world. Instead, the ringing itself changed. It began to waver and undulate and grow in clarity, transforming into clusters of tones. About a year or so after the accident, the invalids began to hear distinct melodic notes.

Signore Lanfranco, a musicologist who happened to be passing through on a visit to an organist in Leipzig, trained some of the invalids to transcribe onto paper the sounds they were hearing. He was astute enough to recognize what no one else could have imagined. Swirling within their ears were distinct musical lines from a single work. Within weeks the town was flooded with theoreticians and contrapuntists, willing to pay every last one of the coins they had coaxed out of their patrons for the chance to teach more of the villagers to transcribe their music. A vast and magnificent expanse could now be glimpsed, one without beginning or end, a masterpiece of polyphony overflowing with themes and counter-themes, motifs and species, exposition and development.

There are few who dare speculate on the origins of this unearthly music. Those who have studied it are unanimous in frustration, because the transcribed portions are monstrous in their incompleteness. The peasants had their stables to clean, their cows to milk, their bread to bake, and little tolerance for the scholars who were intruding into their lives. The most glorious segments are also the most maddening, for they hint at sublime contrapuntal inventions that will never be finished. Composers have tried to deduce the larger structures of this work and fill in its gaps, but their best attempts are nothing compared with the artistry of the original.

The peasants adapted to their deafness, tended to their work, bore healthy children, and ignored the endless march of notes through their ears. No mention of another occurence of this disease has ever been found on the shelves of the Library, nor in the accounts of the many scholars who visit here every day. Many years have passed, and the townsfolk who were infants at the time of the explosion are already aged. The possibility of access to the music has dwindled to a handful of threads. Soon it will diminish to a trio, a duet, a solo.

Mnemosyne's Affliction

Mnemosyne, daughter of Uranus and Gaia and mother of the Muses, presided over memory, while her sister Lesmosyne presided over forgetfulness. Purists believe this affliction ought to take its name from the latter goddess, because it is not, properly speaking, a disease of memory. Rather it deprives its victims of the capacity to forget, which leaves them with a grotesque power.

Mnemosyne's Affliction was discovered in Crete, where a local physician observed a mysterious illness to which the men of a certain family had succumbed for generations. He was the first to describe the characteristic progress of the condition: the extraordinary flowering in the fourth decade of life of a prodigious memory, allowing the invalids to memorize complex documents of governance, book after book of biblical text, extensive lists of numbers from trade ledgers. As time passed they would find themselves remembering not just the contents of their reading but even the shapes of the letters, recalling in perfect detail the boldness of an 'f' or the asymmetry of an 'm'. They could even recall the outlines of stains on the pages they read.

Their faultless recollections would then extend beyond book and text, for every hair and wrinkle on every face they beheld would be burned into their memories, as would the most subtle inflection of every sentence that happened to fall upon their ears. Each tree would become an encyclopedia—the cracks in its rotting bark, the veins on its leaves, the crawl of caterpillars upon its branches, all perfectly catalogued into an unending compendium, along with the colors of pebbles on riverbeds, the motion of individual drops of rain, the chirp and caw of every bird.

While Mnemosyne's Affliction confers incomparable powers of retention on those who inherit it, God seldom grants extraordinary virtues without commanding His tithe. Every other faculty of the mind is displaced by the escalating demands of memory, causing enfeeblement and numbness within the first few years, and unsteadiness and slurred speech by the end of a decade. Within months after that, the disease culminates in the complete loss of all movement, sensation, and expression, and the invalid finally perishes, defeated by the myriad of illnesses to which bodies devoid of government are subject.

The Cretan physician took the liberty of speculating on the mental state of the terminal victim of Mnemosyne's Affliction. While it is impossible to verify his hypothesis, it possesses a macabre plausibility. "It is quite logical to assume," he wrote, "that the invalid with this disease, entombed within his own mind, left with nothing more than the vast repositories of his memory, is forced to remember his own remembrances. His final awareness, before the faculty of thought itself is strangled, must be that of an endless hall of mirrors."

Aevum insolitum

The first known mention of *Aevum insolitum*, or Abnormal Aging, is found in a collection of royal manuscripts from the warriors of the Indian peninsula, which tell of a queen whose chambers were lined with paintings commissioned to immortalize her beauty. The paintings showed her on horseback and in repose, in light and in shadow, in prayer robes and in ceremonial garb. They served as constant reminders of her luminous youth, while she herself advanced into decrepitude. The manuscripts speak of a curse that fell upon her one hot desert night when she ignored a bearded mendicant's plea for alms. On awakening the next morning, she found to her horror that the portraits had aged overnight and were now marred with the wrinkles that etched her skin in life.

As more and more aristocrats seek to immortalize themselves through portraiture, the disease is occurring with greater frequency, though it is brought to the attention of the medical fraternity only rarely. The afflicted often attribute it to sorcery and seek the counsel of exorcists rather than physicians. Even within the medical fraternity, debate continues as to whether this anomaly falls within the purview of medicine, for there are some who argue that the lack of symptoms in the sufferer's physical body relegates it to some other branch of study. However, some consider *Aevum insolitum* to be a disorder of the aging process, whereby it extends its influence beyond the *corpus* and the *anima* into their external representations.

Every bust and portrait of the invalid is altered instantaneously and seamlessly by *Aevum insolitum*. From the moment of infection the images age in step with the person they portray, growing frail and scoliotic and mottled with time, until finally they take on the dull taut complexion of death. There the changes stop, and while the desecration of every family portrait with a waxy corpse is horrific, one must consider it fortunate that *Aevum insolitum* spares its onlookers a glimpse into the process of putrefaction.

The rarity of *Aevum insolitum* hampers attempts to dissect its nature. Confusing the matter further are reports that the disease can extend far beyond the domain of images. Old lists and ledgers fished from the attics of the afflicted show not the bold firm script of youth but the slurred scribbles of arthritic hands. Love letters penned in adolescence lose the gushing affection they once contained and instead breathe a tragic and lonely fatalism.

Visio determinata

Visio determinata, or Finite Vision, imposes a malicious and stringent set of privations upon its sufferers. It is not surprising that most people with the disease cannot comply with their treatment and progress rapidly to the profound blindness that marks its final form. Neither balm nor lamentation can then restore what has forever been lost.

Light itself is damaging to the eyes of those with *Visio determinata,* so that the very act of seeing causes their sight to degenerate. A slight blurring of distant vision begins in late adolescence, when the membranes of the eyes become susceptible to the noxious effects of illumination. The damage is slow at first. The eyesight deteriorates with each exposure to noonday fields, blazing bonfires, sparkling fireworks. After this early damage, if visual gluttony continues, every new injury leads to a precipitous decline, until the invalid can barely find his way around his own home. The final insult that tips him into complete blindness is often the simplest of sights: the glow of an infant's cheek, the tint of an autumn leaf, the gentle red of a robin's breast.

The only remedy for this condition is an impossibly demanding one. The eyes of the invalids must be bound in thick fabric, day and night, tied with such care that it does not slip even during sleep. Blind before their time, the invalids must learn to measure distances in foot lengths, test the solidity of the ground before every step, know the location of a carriage from the clip-clop of hooves. They must memorize the positions of objects they can no longer see: spice pots on shelves, chairs in rooms, trees in yards. They must teach their fingers not only the alphabet of the blind but also the tactile languages of emotion and intimacy. Only thus can they hope to preserve their fragile vision, that they might have it at hand in times of danger, while keeping it bottled for the remainder of their lives.

This condition drives men to madness: a few by the loss of sight itself, but many more by the extraordinary temptations they must resist to preserve it. Some, in fits of despair, stare at the sun until it rids them of both their sight and the burden of preserving it. Others, however, succeed in living with tremendous austerity. At carefully rationed intervals, they reward themselves by unwrapping their blindfolds and feasting on the stars in a moonless sky, a painting in a darkened room, the candlelit body of their beloved. Sometimes, on the rarest of occasions, they may even allow themselves to gorge on the palette of a sunset.

Auditio cruciabilis

Towns infected by *Auditio cruciabilis* are blanketed in silence. The only sound in their streets is that of the wind. The houses appear abandoned, haunted, until one notices the inhabitants tiptoeing in the shadows with scarves wrapped around their ears.

Auditio cruciabilis perverts the hearing of its victims and converts all sounds to stabs of pain. At the first touch of contagion, the town fills with screams. In taverns and granaries, in markets and guildhalls, people cup their ears in agony. The cries die down when they realize that only silence can stop their misery. A terrible new world unfolds before them, one in which utensils must not be clattered, dough not be pounded, nails not be hammered. A world that mires even the act of walking in agony, for any twig might be a source of torture. Song and gossip, laughter and quarrel cease. Even the animals, who are not immune to the torments of *Auditio cruciabilis*, stop their howling and grunting. Perhaps the contagion makes their lives safer. The act of slaughter, rarely possible in silence, becomes anathema.

Such towns fall into ruin and can easily starve. Neighboring villages, recognizing the torments of the disease, leave baskets of food at their outskirts. The invalids usually return the baskets with grateful gifts—coins, jewels, heirlooms. Sometimes they return them with swaddled infants. Infants that wouldn't stop crying.

Few reports exist of the inner workings of these towns. Some scholars claim to have crept across their borders in secret. They write with wonder of the elaborate ballet of the people, the slow, viscous movements they conduct with wary grace, the extraordinary steps they take to preserve the silence.

Toxins that deafen the ears cost more than gold. Those who cannot pay drip wax on their eardrums.

But these towns are fated to die out. They shun the act of procreation, fraught as it is with sounds of pleasure and pain. As the victims succumb to the poisons of age, the silence that envelops the town becomes one of desolation.

Morbus geographicus

The victim of *Morbus geographicus* complains of a cluster of unrelated symptoms: edema of the limbs, spasms of the gut, inflammation of the lungs. His physicians, perplexed, refer him to experts in other towns. The symptoms wax and wane as the invalid makes his travels. Few practitioners know of this disorder, and years may pass without a diagnosis. At last a rare physician who is trained in both cartography and medicine takes the time to comb through the documentation of his peers and find correlations between each symptom and the town in which it was recorded. He refers to maps and charts, compasses and scales, and after careful triangulation prescribes the land that will bring relief to the sufferer.

Morbus geographicus allots its victims a radius on earth within which they may thrive. Any travel beyond its boundaries makes the symptoms recur. The locations are unpredictable. A farmer may be banished to a barren and salty plain, a man of letters to an illiterate village, a councilman to a mountain where he can only preside over wild goats. It is there, however, that the invalid must rebuild his life, fenced in by his disease.

But the initial migration does not cure *Morbus geographicus.* New pains arise with time, and the invalid must then travel to neighboring towns and record the precise intensity of each symptom at each location. He must send these details to the cartographer-physician, who uses them to calculate that the allotted region, for reasons unknown, has shifted. The invalid, in order to soothe his new ills, must detach himself from the land in which he had begun to take root and migrate as *Morbus geographicus* commands. He must cross oceans and continents, pass through lands whose languages he does not speak and whose customs he does not understand, and at last accept the melancholy task of settling into a new house, pretending that its walls will protect him from the world, when in reality the germ of disease within him turns every wall on earth to paper. The invalid becomes a palimpsest, his life etched with layer upon layer of new scenery, until he wonders if there is anything beneath it all. And then one day the trajectory folds in on itself and leads him back to the land of his birth, announcing the end of both his travels and his existence.

VII.

Look how late it's become! My eyesight isn't what it used to be—I have trouble reading in dim light. For obvious reasons, candles and lamps aren't allowed in here.

I'm very pleased that you will work for us here, Máximo. I see in you someone with skills the Library will find valuable. Your experience as an apothecary is unique. Most of our librarians only have a theoretical knowledge of medicine, which limits their understanding of the *Encyclopaedia*. And you have an affliction yourself. Not a life-threatening one, God be thanked, but one that I'm sure you've found crippling at times. It will connect the abstract nature of your work to the truth of human suffering.

Let's walk out this way. The guards will be locking the hall soon.

I fear—I don't mind sharing this with you—I fear for the future of the Library. The *Encyclopaedia* has a structure, yes, but when you wander through the rest of the Library, you'll see more chaos than order. Uncatalogued books and scrolls by the tens of thousands. To sort them we librarians must first read them, understand their contents. But the numbers have grown unmanageable.

The *Encyclopaedia* isn't complete—far from it—yet it's already growing outdated. In a few years, scholars will begin calling for a newer edition. Guilds of physicians will descend on the Library, ransack the treatises piling out there in the corridors, and decide which ones ought to be incorporated into the newer edition. How many volumes will it have? Five hundred? A thousand? How many pelts will go into sewing its pages? One day, I fear, the separate strands will refuse to twist together anymore. The golden thread will unravel. The stacks out in the corridor will overflow the Library and become impossible to curate. The *Encyclopaedia* will lose its authority, and all our knowledge will disperse into fragments. The greatest threat to the *Encyclopaedia*, Máximo, is not a madman with a tinderbox—that's all I'm trying to say.

But enough of that. I don't know why I'm filling your mind with these ideas on your first day here. We librarians are not always this somber. You should take a look at the room where we keep our books on poisons. Along one wall is a bust of Socrates the Greek, forced to face those books for all eternity. We have our manner of humor.

Your room should be ready. Dinner will be in the refectory. You know your way, right? God willing, I will see you tomorrow, and we can talk some more.